Guardian Angel Files 2:
Kindred Spirits

By Julie C. Gilbert

Aletheia Pyralis Publishers

http://www.juliecgilbert.com/
https://sites.google.com/view/juliecgilbert-writer/

Love Science Fiction or Mystery?

Choose your adventure!

Visit: http://www.juliecgilbert.com/

For details on getting
Ashlynn's Dreams and The Kiverson Case
absolutely free

Dedication:

To Amy, without you the idea of Kindred Spirit Bonds
would have been a minor footnote.

And to Francesca and Reuben Corbett who know
exactly why birds are portrayed as demons.

Table of Contents:

What's Gone on Before?
(Warning: Contains spoilers for Spirit's Bane)

In *Spirit's Bane*, two young guardian angels in training, Allister and Mina, discover they share a Kindred Spirit Bond. The connection magnifies their Gifts and allows them to use each other's abilities, but it also draws unwanted attention from Satan and his top lieutenants.

Mina gets captured and held in a spirit prison. Meanwhile, demons attack the Academy and carry off students and teachers, taking them to another prison on Forsaken Island. Allister has two nearly impossible tasks: find Mina and rescue the other angels.

Hadeon, Satan's Director of Operations, places a weapon called Spirit's Bane around Mina's neck to keep her in human form long enough to kill. He aims to show off its abilities through the execution before using the prototype to create more of the weapon.

He chose the wrong victim. Mina is perhaps the only angel who can resist the evil device due to her healing abilities and Allister's Gifts of Transportation and Teleportation.

Joined by many other angels, Allister and Mina battle Satan's forces to a stalemate and rescue everybody taken to Forsaken Island.

Mina chooses to keep Spirit's Bane until it can be

destroyed, rather than risk it falling into the wrong hands.

Part 1:
Process

Prologue:
Patience

Dear Than,

I know you are eager to impress me but be cautious about the number of correspondences you risk. Every contact increases the chances of making a fatal mistake. My plans to send you backup are progressing, but unforeseen circumstances have delayed them.

Your orders have not changed. Continue to humbly offer your services as an intermediate for the girl. The Council of Light likely wants to give Mina time to adjust to her new circumstances before granting her an official assignment. It has only been a few weeks in the mortal realm.

In answer to your question, no, you should not say anything regarding the boy's petition to become the girl's liaison with the Heavens. I told you that would happen. Trust the Council of Light's innate sense of caution to prevail. Allister's impatience will serve us well in the long game, but for now, it is of no consequence. Focus on gathering information, directing your existing forces, and inserting new demons into their assigned locations.

Since you've had success with encouraging the demons under your command to imitate and inhabit small creatures, consider expanding to larger ones. Birds have always performed well as extra eyes, but if you wish to infiltrate homes, you will need domesticated animals. You'll have to experiment. Rabbits might seem like a good choice, but they tend not to be given free rein of the house. Dogs are naturally trusting, but demons might not take too well to that much exposure. Cats might be the better choice simply because they're more mysterious. Erratic behavior would be easier to explain in this form.

When the time comes to finish the Spirit's Bane business with Mina, I will let you know. If you are free, I will allow you to participate, but you must have patience. The weapon shall continue to carry out the Dark Master's will regardless of there being a presence to direct it. In other words, if the girl imprisons Spirit's Bane long enough in her human form, it shall have its revenge upon her.

Do not worry about the boy. Leave him to Daeva. She has become quite committed to his downfall. If she seeks your aid, give it to her without reservation.

Perhaps one day we can use the boy and girl against each other, but for now, I am gratified that the Council keeps them apart. Nevertheless, I expect everybody to consider how to contain and control the Kindred Spirit Pair should they reunite. The bond itself may grow to allow their powers to be amplified even over a distance. We simply do not know enough about it. If you can do it quietly, research such connections in the Grand Library and get back to me with anything you learn. We must know more to avoid underestimating the bond again.

Spirit's Bane could give us the advantage we need. It must be recovered. My message to you is the same as to many others right now. Be subtle. Be persistent. Be persuasive. Every soul counts. The more people you corrupt, the more likely it is that you will draw out the guardians. Eventually, somebody will lead us to the girl. Unimaginable power and prestige await the demon or demons who can deliver her to me.

Do not be afraid to work together. There is enough glory to go around. I know you have reservations about trusting Deimos, but he answers to me and the Dark Master, not you. Remember that and stay out of his way. He's in the middle of a delicate mission. If he requires aid, render it. We are strong because we are many.

The Guilt demons I assigned to the girl have not yet reported in. Once we can establish communications with them, feed them as many stories as you can. Consider pursuing the young angels you rescued during the Academy affair. Aderes, Osmund, and Adelmo have worked with the angelings before. If we can lay enough pain and destruction at their feet, Mina and Allister may let their egos overrule their common sense.

The angelings have both shown a distinct weakness for tactics involving threats against others, but such traps will be harder to set in the future because they are aware of our knowledge. Still, every connection counts, so form bonds of friendship with both of them if you can. That would require finding the girl, of course, but do not worry about that at this time. She will be found eventually.

As stated previously: do not waver.

And beat that message into those who answer to you. The girl's foolish notion of the path of light being open to recent recruits is dangerous. Besides, this war isn't about the servants of light or dark. It's about Earth. We must prevail there if we hope to bring our Master the glory he deserves and, in turn, receive the glory due us.

I do not have many leads for you since your last inquiry was yesterday, but I will pass on what came in this morning's briefing.

Callum Hennessey's depression has progressed nicely. He's nearing a point where a few casual thoughts of suicide may prove fruitful.

Tyson Green has an official guardian and will be very hard to approach from now on, but you may want to assign somebody to monitor the situation anyway. His

Siphon abilities could come in handy. Generally, direct conflict with guardians should be avoided, but he may be worth fighting for.

Dalilah Youssef is taking her brother's death poorly. Seize the opportunity.

Guard your heart and mind against temptation. The path of light leads to weakness.

I will send Aridam to you soon. When he arrives, turn over some your day to day duties to him and concentrate on the Kindred Spirit problem.

Hadeon, Servant of the Dark Master,
Director of Operations

Chapter 1:
Official Assignment

Case Report #: MN-115
Case Agents: Master Blaz and Mistress Codee
Guardian: Mina Nadir

I miss Allister. If he ever reads this report, he'll tease me about that, but I don't care. This is harder than I thought it would be. It's one thing to understand the rightness of a path and another matter to walk it.

I also miss my spirit form, but I must not dwell on that. There are many good things about the situation. Being deprived of something gives one a deeper appreciation for the missing item or ability. In addition, remaining abilities become honed and enhanced out of necessity. For now, I cannot utilize my Gift for easily switching forms between human, twilight state, and full spirit. On the other hand, being confined to my human body has forced me to explore the extent to which I can access my talents in this form. Previously, if I wanted to heal or use one of Allister's Gifts, I would switch to spirit, but I discovered that I can still access some Gifts without such a shift.

Although I've been on Earth for a few weeks, I have not yet attended school. I will have to soon though because this country requires school attendance. Mistress Codee has already registered me at the local high school. We discussed the issue of grade at length and finally settled on sophomore or tenth grade. My human form could pass for anything from fourteen to eighteen if I wish, but I tend to prefer features that favor the younger ages.

Mistress Codee has lived up to her name in being helpful during this time. Despite a strongly worded letter from the school, she insisted I spend several days acclimating to the limitations of being human. The most difficult thing to get used to thus far has been being physically weary. Even during my month-long training on Earth, I subtly shifted enough to renew myself as needed. I would do so now if I wasn't trying to hide my presence from demons and avoid the burning pain of Spirit's Bane.

The necklace still occupies its innocent form. The design is simple, elegant, and even beautiful. There's a small, flower-shaped diamond in the pendant's center. The circular frame making up the pendant is gold. Thin strands of gold flow toward the center, creating several flower shapes with the blank spaces. The entire thing easily fits across the span of three fingers. Every time I look at it, I'm reminded of how attractive evil things can be. No wonder humans struggle so much.

Waiting and walking are two more things I needed to adjust to. Even the briefest exposure to Allister's Teleportation Gift spoiled me. Waiting is still difficult, but I have come to enjoy walking outside. Nature, even muted as it is in suburban North America, shines with praise to the Glorious King. It's currently the Fall season and many trees are entering the part of their cycle where their leaves change colors before dying. It's fascinating, yet sad.

Mistress Codee's house stands slightly apart from the nearest neighbors. There's a short path behind the house that leads to a garden and a little stream. The stream has become my favorite place to sit and think. Mistress Codee has warned me at least twice to wear a jacket. I keep forgetting because my body doesn't register the discomfort of cold temperatures like a normal human.

I'm not complaining, but I do occasionally wonder why my human body seems more efficient, for lack of a better term, than the natural humans.

When I posed the question to Mistress Codee, her presence brightened with amusement. I expected her to dismiss the question, but instead, she answered with the deep wisdom I've come to love about her.

"You have come from the presence of the King. That might seem like a small thing, but it has marked you in a big way." She then drew me into a hug and encouraged my spirit.

I'm surprised I could sense that even while in human form. It's what alerted me to the fact that staying as a human might not leave me as helpless as I thought it would.

I have not experimented to the extent that I must, but so far, I have ruled out using most flashy supernatural Gifts like Teleportation—moving persons—and Transportation—moving objects. That may only be because those Gifts originate with Allister or it might be due to my lack of experience with using them. An encounter with a sharp rock showed me some of my healing abilities still work. Mistress Codee says I'll need to consciously control that when around mortals.

Something tells me Allister and I have not discovered all our Gifts. I know that sounds greedy. Many angels only receive one or two talents to aid them with their duties.

My ability to sense things about a person remains intact. It's a kind of Empathy. Of my Gifts, this one probably manifested first, but my early training did not provide many opportunities to use it. I get the feeling my new assignment will have me using it quite regularly. Can't say I imagined my first official guardian posting being in a high school, but it makes sense considering my limitations thanks to Spirit's Bane. So far, I've come up blank on how to deal with that, but there should be time to ponder the problem in the coming months.

I've begun my work by praying. Hill Crest High School has not had a guardian for several years. Many places never receive a guardian because one is not asked for. Mortals, Americans especially, cling to the idea that they must be self-sufficient to prove their worth. The hundreds of thousands of prayers that flow into the Heavens each day ought to be many times more than that. I know a guardian could be assigned without an official request, but it's much easier to work in a place with open hearts and minds.

According to the file, the petitioner, a girl in tenth grade by the name of Kyrie Eleison Rostam, is a new Christian. Her cry for help stemmed from the fear she would fall back into the old ways, ruled by thoughts of appearance and self. I look forward to meeting her in person. My schedule will have to be adjusted if I am to stay near her, but the description of the assignment expands my responsibilities to the entire school of 1304 souls, including students, faculty, and staff. It's a daunting task, but one I'm grateful for. I was afraid the Council would withhold a real assignment until the weapon I wear has been dealt with.

In a way, I am eager for the chance to fully walk the human path. If anything could convince me I still have much to learn, it's this. Perhaps, I finally understand the notion of strength shining brighter through weakness. That thought might only be wishful thinking.

Many guardians spend much of their careers watching over a single soul from first to final breath. I say this not to boast but to point out why a buzzing fear has gripped me. It's half-anticipation and half-terror.

1304.

I'm not sure how to handle my new assignment. Do I work subtly to touch each life at the surface or identify a few needs and fix them? Time and space constraints will prevent me from encountering everybody physically. I can perhaps reach them spiritually, but I must be cautious not to subconsciously change forms if I do that.

It's so tempting. Every time I let my thoughts wander, I long to feel the freedom of spirit form.

I must concentrate.

What manner of opposition will I face? I anticipate encounters with Guilt, Pride, Anger, Sloth, Fear, Lust, and Jealousy demons, but will there be others?

Master Blaz's statement about categorizing demons by their primary job being unfair sticks with me. Angels and demons aren't so different. We only serve different masters. They will have different abilities in their arsenals, so I must be ready for anything.

The enemy speaks an attractive message to humans and angels alike.

You deserve to be a god.

Not sure if that message comes from Spirit's Bane or

remains from my brief time in captivity. I lay it out here because holding it in may give it a chance to grip my mind and heart. Truly, I do not know what role I am to play in the larger war, but I know whom I serve.

Mistress Codee asked how I intend to fulfill my guardian duties without revealing myself to the demons. For some reason, Satan and Hadeon have not forgotten me. I'd sort of hoped they would focus on a new scheme by now. On the other hand, I would not wish their malevolent attention upon anyone.

The quick answer to Mistress Codee's query is this: hide in plain sight.

I need a plan of action.

My first task upon reaching the school will be to bind the demons brazen enough to have taken up a permanent residence there. That should keep the word in for a time. Next, I'll bolster the prayer barriers and establish clear perimeters. The tiny patch of land will be claimed for my King. The demons who travel into the school like parasites on the people will be dealt with accordingly. If I stick to prayers and truth only, they may not even recognize me as an angel.

It's not a permanent solution, but it is a viable start.

I must also prepare and protect my heart. Knowledge is power, but it can also be heartbreaking and heavy. The scant glimpses of people's problems and burdens during my Prayer Room tours of duty showed me that much. While watching from the Heavens I could observe yet remain detached. The luxury of detachment will no longer exist for me.

As I fall into the nightly wind-down routine, I silently pray.

Dear Glorious King, lend me strength for the tasks ahead. You have equipped me to protect these precious ones, both claimed and unclaimed. Guide my words and actions. May each victory, great or small, further establish your domain on Earth.

Chapter 2:
I Am Ready

Case Report #: AK-115
Case Agent: Mistress Adira Clarimond
Guardian: Allister Knight
Today could have gone better.

I feel like I've been here before. The office I'm in certainly offers more legroom than the Academy's interrogation suite or Lady A.'s office there. I slump in the comfy chair, feeling hollow. My body still aches from the rigors of Blaz's latest obstacle course. Dried sweat makes my fingers tacky. I could switch to spirit form or call a fresh set of clothes, but what's the point? Smelling better won't change my scores.

If I were still an Academy student, I might be dismissed from the program outright. Now that I've received my commission, the worst that could happen is a recommendation for remedial training. I'm sort of getting that anyway since my situation is *unique*. I'm starting to dislike that word.

Across from me, Mistress Adira Clarimond wears her unreadable expression. For a while, she keeps silent, leaving some time for my thoughts to run fine circles around each other. I know she could read them if she so desired, but I don't think she's accessing that Gift right now. Her relaxed posture indicates she's waiting me out.

"I am ready," I say, hoping to spark some response.

Lady A.'s expression remains completely devoid of clues

as she watches me.

"What would you like me to say, Allister?" Her question catches me off-guard.

"The Council came to its senses and assigned me to wherever they've sent Mina," I answer.

Mina would scold me for the flippant answer.

I brace for Lady A.'s anger. Instead, she laughs.

"Give us time," she replies. "I will present your request upon our next meeting."

"You agree with me?" I can't keep the shock out of my voice. I sit up straighter.

"Why is that hard to believe?" Her mild tone contains a hint of curiosity, though I suspect she already knows my answer.

"I ... guess I assumed the Council's decision would be unanimous," I reply.

"I would have thought witnessing the discussion over whether to give you and Mina your commissions would have cured you of that notion," Lady A. comments with a gentle smile. "Aside from the discovery of a demon amongst us, that was a typical meeting."

Her statement draws a question out of me.

"Have they found Master Josiah?" A dose of guilt moves through me at having completely forgotten about Master Josiah Delshad. For the enemy to successfully replace him, they must have captured him.

"No, would you like to help with that?"

Once again, Lady A. surprises me.

"How can I help?" I'm not looking for praise. I genuinely don't know how one would even begin such a search.

Her gaze sharpens as she seriously considers the offer.

"Your Gift for thinking forward would be invaluable in locating him," Lady A. says.

My enthusiasm for the task wanes, followed by another wave of guilt. I don't need a Guilt demon around; my emotions are very good at conjuring the feeling. If I can help Master Josiah, I should, but I'd envisioned a lot more action in a first assignment. The idea of sitting in a room discussing where to send others isn't very appealing.

"This isn't a desperate bid to keep you from danger,"

Lady A. assures me. "Though I'll admit that aspect would please me." She sighs. "Besides, everyone on the team will likely play a part in the rescue when that time comes."

"Even me?" My question is a challenge.

"You're a Guardian, Allister," Lady A. says. "If we've done our jobs well, you should be able to handle yourself in most situations, but an abundance of natural Gifts and great skill in employing them does not make you invincible. You still need help, and we still need your help."

My eyes fall shut as I absorb her mild rebuke.

"What do you require of me?" I automatically insert formality into my question, sensing the gravity of the moment.

"First, an explanation for your performance in the obstacle course today." There's no trace of condemnation in her tone, but she's back to watching me closely. "Do you believe the scores are accurate?"

That's a tricky question.

Lady A. has given me an opening to protest the scores. While harsh at a few points, they're probably accurate enough. I can't even work up enough emotion to be angry with an unfair call or two. I conclude that the scores don't mean much to me anyway, besides being a point of pride. That gets me thinking about why Blaz suggested I run the course today.

What's the point?

"It's not about the score," I murmur, coming to the realization as the words leave my mouth.

Lady A. looks intrigued, but she waits for me to continue.

"This was a test," I conclude. "What was my real score?"

"A bit higher than what was reported," Lady A. admits. "But not as high as it should be and nowhere near your usual scores. Why do you suppose that is?"

"I'm missing a part of myself." The admission contains painful truth, but it's not the whole truth. Frustrated, I shake my head. "It's more than that. I need to be with Mina. I have to protect her. I hate feeling so …"

"Helpless," Lady A. finishes.

It's not exactly the word I was going for, but it'll do.

I nod curtly then sigh.

"I understand that Mina and I won't always work

together, but this is different," I say. "I should be with her now. She shouldn't have to face Spirit's Bane alone."

"She's not alone," Lady A. replies, "but I see your point. Be patient. This is a new situation for everybody. And this is a dangerous time for us. The Council is weighing many options for handling the increased demon activity." Her calm exterior cracks enough for me to see the worry in her eyes.

"But we win, right?" I ask, unsettled by her worry.

"The end is not the question." Lady A.'s voice has comforting certainty in it this time as well as some deep wisdom. "Our Glorious King will absolutely triumph, but that doesn't make it easier to watch friends bear the burdens they are asked to carry."

I gather she's speaking of more than my situation.

"Did you … know Master Josiah well?" I wonder.

"We trained together at the Academy," Lady A. says. "And we've participated in some of the same missions over the centuries. He too has a Gift for thinking forward. That's why he was a natural choice to be on the Council of Light."

"Why do you think they went after him?" I ask, hoping I'm not going too far. It has to be more than thinking forward. It's a useful Gift, but it can't actually predict the future. "If I'm to help, I need to know as much as possible."

"You don't have to justify the question," Lady A. assures me. "It is a fair one. And in answer: I'm not sure. It's something you'll have to discuss at length with Valin and Aderes soon. They've been given this task as well."

"That's it?" I'm surprised by the small number for such an important mission.

"If you need more help, ask Blaz, Ranger, or Reena, but I'm trying to minimize the number of participants," Lady A. says. "I'm not exactly sure who can be trusted and who cannot."

"What makes you trust us?" The dumb question slips out before I can stop it.

"I believe the demons would have a hard time imitating you." Lady A. tries half-heartedly to suppress a small smile. "As for the others, I have cleared them myself. And before you ask, yes, I think you should test me." Standing, she holds out a hand toward me as if I should shake it.

I stare stupidly at her trying to guess if she's serious. She looks sincere. If she was a demon replacement, could she create a shield for her hand? My gaze lingers on her hand.

Following my thoughts, Lady A. folds her hands in front of her body.

"Run whatever test you like, Allister."

At her second prompt, I freeze time, flip to spirit, and microjump through Lady A.'s physical form. She recovers in time to prevent me from passing through her, but instead of doing so, she shifts to spirit and allows the brief contact. It feels like moving through a stiff breeze. It's almost the same test that revealed the demon imposter of Master Josiah, but Lady A. passes perfectly.

The contact between our spirits lasts no more than a second, but it gives me first-hand experience with Lady A.'s determination to find her friends. There's definitely more than one being she's searching for. I get no more insights on the other missing friend's identity, only a vague notion that the person is connected to Master Josiah.

"When you find him, let me know," Lady A. instructs, once she's back in human form.

I let my spirit form fade and solidify my physical being.

"I will help you plan the rescue and prepare a team," Lady A. continues. "The question of our participation in that operation is one for later. If you truly feel ready to accept this assignment, meet the others in the library. Aderes will reach out when you leave the office."

To my surprise, Lady A. draws me into a quick hug.

"Be careful. The enemy will not fight fair." She releases me but keeps her left hand on my right shoulder. "Trust in the King. You have the power and strength you need to succeed."

Chapter 3:
Holy Ground

Case Report #: MN-116
Case Agents: Master Blaz and Mistress Codee
Guardian: Mina Nadir

School on Earth differs a lot from the Academy. For one thing, the Academy has cohorts that take the same main classes with each other. These range in size from about ten students up to about fifty. I guess the Earth-school equivalent would be one class year, consisting of those set to graduate at the same time, but the analogy isn't perfect. The cohort Allister and I started with had thirty-two angels in it, but since individuals can proceed at their own pace, some graduated before us, some changed the course of their lives to pick up other occupations, and some are still studying. We graduated only slightly before the main group. The last few will likely finish with the cohort behind us.

On Earth, you don't get to meet as many people during the course of your studies. At Hill Crest High School there can be as many as thirty students in a humanities core class. The science classes tend to be smaller, but depending on your schedule, you're likely to only see certain students for one or two classes a day.

Having now walked the hallways, I can safely say there's a lot of work to be done. I'm excited but a tad overwhelmed. The schedule can be confusing at first, but I like that they blocked out an hour for most lunch periods, except if you have a science lab.

That will give me a chance to do the majority of my real work.

Before I describe my action plan, it's worth noting that the school's sports teams are known as the comets. Mistress Codee had to explain the notion of mascots to me. The school colors are blue, white, and yellow. One can usually tell who plays sports by their clothes. About a third of the students wear some sort of school apparel. Guess I'll have to look into buying a shirt or two to blend in.

Since Mistress Codee had her choice of about three dozen schools in this region of the country, I doubt it's an accident she chose the one whose mascot consists of comets. It's something I can relate to very well. Comets are celestial pieces of ice and dust that form a distinctive tail as they burn up in the atmosphere of a planet. They're most beautiful when they're burning, yet underneath the fire and bluster, it's still rock dust and ice. I'm humbled and amazed that the Glorious King can take something ungainly and plain and turn it into art.

My first full day at the school revealed a grim situation, but if I remember my studies correctly, it's the same the world over. The overall sense of morale seems strong. Signs in nearly every corner claim the space is a stigma-free safe zone, but that's a lie. Many people wearing bright smiles are barely holding their emotions together. Stress, anxiety, and pain fill the air.

Although I cannot take spirit form, I still benefit from spiritual sight. It's similar to The Sight given to certain descendants of angels who chose to marry mortals in ages past. When accessing this Gift, I gain insight into the primary emotions dominating a person. I suppose everybody works differently.

I like colors, so I assigned each emotion its own unique signature. Stress shows up as some shade of yellow. Anxiety is purple. Pain registers as orange if emotional and red if physical. Evil intent and malicious thoughts are black and gray respectively. Joy and happiness are blue and white. You can imagine the riot of colors in any gathering of people, especially predominantly young ones.

The blended milky blue-white color of peace appears from time to time, but not often. Every time I find it, I look for the seal. Although many who possess peace in any significance do have the seal, a surprising number do not. When I asked Mistress Codee about that, she said these people are in more danger than those bleeding bright colors because it means they're fully invested in the enemy's lies that this world is the beginning and end for them.

I sensed dozens of demons coming and going with various people, but only two took an interest in me, a Guilt demon and an Anxiety demon. Both left me for easier targets once they sensed the King's light upon my soul. Since I resisted the urge to battle them directly, I think my cover's still intact. The Guilt demon seemed philosophical about the strength of my spirit, but the Anxiety demon muttered a curse and promised to return with reinforcements. It's probably an empty threat, but I will be cautious anyway.

Any place touched by the King's presence becomes holy ground. Those who bear his seal or serve him as angels also carry the Holy Messenger in their souls, but my time in the school tells me that Christians often fail to utilize their powers. I'm not sure they understand that they can influence the spiritual realms. At any given moment, there's always a prayer or two being lifted, but these often lack purpose and direction. They're quick, heartfelt cries or wishful missives, not arrows aimed at the enemy.

I hope to change that.

Mistress Codee asked me for my action plan. Don't know how coherent it will be, but here are my initial thoughts.

Since I carry echoes of the King's light within me, I will use my prayer time in the school to open more pockets of holy ground. These should reach out and encourage the citizens of Heaven whether I'm present or not. This assignment won't last forever, and I don't want my work to collapse when I move on.

Next, I will reach out and train the Christians to maintain these locations. I think of them like water fountains capable of delivering spiritual renewal. There's nothing magical about it. A few people discover the ability to tap into places of emotional and spiritual strength instinctively, but direct and indirect training should help make their upkeep easier by spreading out the work. I view direct training as one-to-one purposeful instruction and indirect training as the act of silently showing their spirits how to do the job.

I could clear the school of demons myself, and it's very tempting to do so. However, that would be disastrous in the long run. I won't always be present to fight their battles, so I need to teach the believers how to fight for themselves and those around them. Besides, this school makes up only one aspect of their lives. They each have homes, clubs, sports, and other spheres of influence.

I can't be everywhere at once, though that would be a neat Gift.

If phase one is clearing the land in and around the school and phase two is providing sources of spiritual renewal, I guess the third step would be to create connections between the various believers. Their primary weapons of prayer and encouragement are underutilized. Of these, I believe encouragement will be the harder one to explain to them.

Words are powerful.

People often dismiss words as less potent than actions, yet they naturally wield words as weapons or a means of daily defense. They are taught to use words as an alternative to physical confrontations. While that makes sense, it can be devastating over time. Words do not leave visible wounds, but they can fester inside longer, especially in those who think deeper on such things.

Humans are baffling. Nobody should walk spiritual roads alone. They wouldn't take a dark, twisting, dangerous trail alone at night, yet they often try to forge through unknown spirit lands by themselves. They need each other, whether their physical forms know about each other or not. They have so much potential, yet much of it goes to waste because of perceived embarrassment. Perhaps if I can raise general spiritual awareness I can teach them how to support one another. We'll work up to bolder moves.

As I consider my task, I'm more aware of how much I must learn. The lectures, life lessons, and demonstrations of how demons work don't seem like enough when faced with the reality.

Am I good enough?

That's probably the wrong question. It's easy to want to

assume the burden of responsibility for others, but I must remember, my work enhances what's been done before. It's my privilege to be a part of these people's journey for as long as the time lasts. When I move on, my King will bring another guide into place, leaving me to pick up a new mission. I can't help thinking there's a specific reason the King sent me to Earth. It could be to save millions, but I think it more likely it's to save one soul. I just don't know who that is yet.

Chapter 4:
Emissary

Case Report #: AK-116
Case Agent: Mistress Adira Clarimond
Guardian: Allister Knight

As promised, Aderes met me as I left Lady A.'s office, but I never made it to the meeting. Practically before I got to greet Aderes, Lady A. appears beside us. Her expression doesn't say a lot, but the hesitation before she speaks tells me much.

"Go to the meeting and get it started," Lady A. instructs Aderes. "Have Valin note each of the known spirit prisons on the map and help him narrow down more locations where there could be undocumented prisons. I will send Allister along to the library when I can."

"Yes, Mistress Clarimond," replies Aderes. She bows to both of us before turning to spirit and disappearing through a wall.

Lady A. levels a measuring look at me.

I get the feeling she doesn't want to deliver whatever message she bears.

"What happened?" I ask.

"An emissary arrived at the New York campus of the Academy tonight," Lady A. says.

"Is that unusual?" I wonder. "Will we have to move the campus now that the enemy knows where to find it?"

I avoid the obvious question of why she's telling me

21

because I know I'll get that answer eventually.

"I think they've had the information for a while," Lady A. says. "The bigger issue is the demon's request to see you. He won't say anything more besides the fact that the message will be delivered only to you."

"And you suspect a trap?" The words are mostly statement with a hint of a rhetorical question in them.

"I do," Lady A. confirms, "but I don't know the nature of this trap. It's likely an open invitation for you to avoid much conflict by surrendering. Yet with the interest Lucifer and Hadeon have shown in you, I'd say we should expect anything."

"Will you let me meet this demon?" I ask.

Over the past several seconds, Lady A.'s expression has intensified.

"Under a few conditions, yes," she replies. "One, Blaz and I will be present the whole time. Two, you go nowhere with this emissary, regardless of the promises he makes. And three, you discuss the offer with us should the demon find a way to deliver it solely to you. Do you agree to these terms?"

Lady A. extends a hand toward me, palm up. I could probably teleport wherever I need to go, but it will be easier to let her guide me. Every campus of the Academy consists of several buildings.

"I do." I don't actually have a choice if I want to meet the demon. That much is clear in Lady A.'s stance.

Our hands clasp, but we don't immediately teleport.

"I may keep a hand upon your shoulder during the conversation," Lady A. says. "This has little to do with a lack of faith in your words and more to do with a general mistrust of demons. They rarely have the ability to teleport with others, especially within the Academy, but I am not leaving your safety to chance."

"Do you think he means to cause trouble?" I wonder. "Should you and Master Blaz risk the exposure?"

"Yes, on both accounts," Lady A. answers.

Before I can question her further, she teleports us directly to one of the smaller lecture halls within the Academy's New York campus on Earth. Guess they don't wish to destroy one of the nicer rooms if a fight breaks out.

Master Blaz and the demon emissary are the only other beings present. Although Master Blaz doesn't have a weapon drawn, his scowl says he's gearing up for trouble. He stands in front of the teacher's desk, looking ready to tackle the demon if necessary.

I must be guilty of stereotyping because I did not expect the demon ambassador to have the appearance of a young boy sitting on one of the desks two rows away from Master Blaz. The demon's head swivels toward me, and he stops swinging his legs back and forth. His posture straightens and a bright smile sweeps over his features. The light brown hair and green eyes make him look especially harmless.

Next instant, Tyre's in my hands, and I take a guard position, keeping the broad spirit sword between me and the demon.

He laughs. The sound starts out light and carefree before shifting to a malicious, adult-sounding laugh.

"I thought you might remember me," he comments, affecting an appropriate tone that matches the boy's form. "I've missed this form."

"What's a Despair demon doing playing messenger?" I demand.

"Put the sword away, Allister," Lady A. says, squeezing my right shoulder gently. "He is our guest for the moment."

It's clear that could change any second.

"This is the demon that tormented Crystal Benson." My clipped tone brims with anger. Crystal's distressed face appears in my mind. During my training, I had to fight this Despair demon to prevent her from committing suicide.

"I know, but that is over now." Lady A.'s voice washes over me in calming waves. "You ended that torment. Allowing him to provoke you gives him power he does not deserve."

The Despair demon hops off the desk and takes the form of an old man carrying a cane.

"Listen to your elder, child," he advises in an appropriately aged voice.

"Enough games," snaps Master Blaz. "Deliver your message."

The demon rapidly changes forms appearing as Master

Blaz, Lady A., me, Mina, and Master Josiah before finally settling back to his natural state of thick, black smoke.

"I beg to differ on the subject of games," says the demon. His words come out in a harsh, vicious whisper. "My Master invites everybody to play with him." He flashes through the faces in the same order again. "One will suffer. One will fail. One will perish. One will triumph, and one will despair. Which is which? Time will tell."

"What does that mean?" I wonder.

"Claim the first turn, and you shall see," promises the demon.

"I think we're done," Lady A. declares. "Blaz, please see our guest out."

The black smoke scatters in several directions, but the demon's voice still comes from the same location.

"That's not very sporting," he complains. His "s" sounds drag out longer than they should, making the words more sinister. "The offer to Allister is genuine."

"What offer?" I know I shouldn't ask the question, but I do anyway.

"Be the hero. Come to us and choose who lives," says the demon. The smoke coalesces again, and he takes on Master Josiah's form. "Will you save this one?" Another shift gives him Mina's features again. "Or this one?" He saunters forward slowly still channeling my friend. "We know of your feelings for her."

I stare transfixed. Even though I know the face to be a lie, the sight sparks a longing within me.

"Allister, you must go," Lady A. says urgently. She tugs on my shoulder until I stumble back a step before slipping around me. Tamotsu, Lady A.'s katana, springs out of the Veil as a shield forms around me. "Now."

Instinctively, I revert back to my last location, the space outside Lady A.'s Council office. Frustrated, I lose my concentration and land on my knees. Tyre clanks down beside me. I pound both fists on the ground, snatch up my sword, spring to my feet, and prepare to dive back into the fray, but before I can move Lady A. and Master Blaz appear beside me.

A groan escapes Master Blaz, and he leans heavily against the wall to my right. Lady A. catches him. I send Tyre back into the Veil and help Lady A. lower Master Blaz's human form to the floor.

"Demon's gone," Master Blaz mumbles with a weak smile. His face is bright red and starting to blister. He must not have a strong healing Gift or else he'd likely flip over to spirit form to let his human body rest.

"What do you mean?" I sound breathless.

"Well, that was different," Lady A. mutters. Kneeling next to Master Blaz, she cups her hands around his face and begins the healing process.

I wait impatiently, giving her time to work in peace. A dozen questions burn in my chest. When I look closer, I notice that the burns cover every visible part of Master Blaz. Even Lady A.'s hands and arms look red, though I can't see her face from this angle.

What could do that to them?

Lady A. continues to heal Master Blaz and answers my unspoken question.

"The demon exploded into pure corruption. There was nothing to fight, and we failed to get out of the way quickly enough."

One will suffer. One will despair.

The demon's taunt comes back to me.

Lady A. glares up at me fiercely.

"Don't believe a word of that."

"But it came true," I argue, half-heartedly.

"If this didn't happen, something else would convince you," Master Blaz explains. The red color slowly fades as the burns heal. "Don't take them to heart."

"We need to warn Mina," I say, ignoring Master Blaz's advice. "The demon showed us her face too."

Lady A. straightens and catches my arm before I can teleport anywhere.

"You don't know where she is, and it's likely that the demon's goal was to drive you to her side," she says. "Go to the meeting and help Valin and Aderes with a plan to find Master Josiah. Let me worry about getting a message to Mina."

"What's the point?" I argue. "I could walk up to any demon and demand to be taken to Master Josiah."

"You'd wind up a prisoner alongside him," Master Blaz says. He sounds tired. "Not a stellar plan." He rests his head back on the floor. "When I'm back on my feet, we can return to the Academy and make sure the corruption hasn't spread."

"Blaz—" Lady A. begins.

"You sent for security already," says Master Blaz. "We'll only be observing the cleanup and pitching in where we can." His tone moves from matter-of-fact to concerned. "He needs this, Adira."

Although I hate being discussed while present, I keep quiet while we wait for Lady A.'s response. She looks exasperated, which I take as a good sign.

"Make it quick," she says at last, directing the statement to Master Blaz before turning a stern gaze on me. "I still want you to help with Master Josiah."

"Why?" I wonder, thinking over the others in our little committee. "We're not exactly the most experienced angels."

Valin's got a reputation as a hotshot, and my brief time working near Aderes says she's competent. Still, even if we added up the months of our experience as full guardians, it probably doesn't make a year. I didn't even know Aderes had earned her commission, and mine happened mere weeks ago.

"We need fresh minds tackling the assignment," Lady A. answers. "I have asked a few 'more experienced' people to think on the matter as well, but I'm interested in what you can come up with on your own before comparing notes to those already working the problem."

By this time, the skin of Master Blaz's human form has healed completely.

I help him stand.

"How many angels are involved?" I wonder, recalling Lady A.'s previous statement about keeping the number of participants low.

"Who said they were all angels?" Lady A. responds.

"I ... didn't think humans got involved in our affairs," I say.

"A threat to any life deserves our full effort," says Master Blaz in his teaching voice. "But this is slightly more urgent. As a Council member, Master Josiah knows of the identities of countless agents, some of whom are deep under cover."

"He wouldn't betray us willingly," Lady A. says quickly. "But everybody has a breaking point. We must find him soon."

Chapter 5:
Pie and People

Case Report #: MN-117
Case Agents: Master Blaz and Mistress Codee
Guardian: Mina Nadir

As I step through the front door, I sense something wrong. Normally, I'd switch forms and summon Kentaro, my spirit sword. Instead, I let my backpack slide down my right arm to the floor and cautiously approach the kitchen. The second's delay allows me to further analyze my feeling. It's not sounding a danger alarm, but Mistress Codee is distressed.

"Come in, Mina," says Mistress Codee. "You need to hear this."

Entering the kitchen, I find Mistress Codee sitting across from another angel. The guest looks up, causing recognition to blossom inside me.

"What are you doing here?" My cheeks flush, and I scramble to say something less confrontational. Allister must be rubbing off on me. "I'm sorry. I mean it's nice to see you, but I didn't expect to see anyone familiar so soon."

Something big must have happened for one of the Council of Light members to seek me out.

"Nothing has changed with your assignment," Lady A. assures me, "but there is a new threat you should know about."

I stare at Mistress Adira Clarimond. Since when have I taken to thinking of her as *Lady A.*? During training, she was

Allister's mentor, so it makes sense that he would address her informally, but she and I have a very different relationship.

"You may address me as you like." Lady A. waves to one of the free chairs at the table. "I must leave soon, but I am leaving you a memory capsule to help explain the latest development. Elizabeth can answer some of your questions when you finish with the thoughts."

Lady A. stands and nods to the table where a small round sphere appears in the fruit basket.

Her use of Lady Codee's first name surprises me. I wasn't aware they knew each other well enough to dispense with formalities. I'm also not used to her reading my surface thoughts, but I think she has always had that Gift.

"How is Allister? Does he know about the threat?"

I can answer the second question myself. Of course, he knows. It probably revolves around him. My friend was never much for keeping out of trouble.

"He's not pleased with the current arrangements," Lady A. says. "And to be honest, I'm not either. I suspect the answers we seek may require full use of your combined efforts. That won't happen if you're kept apart."

"Has the Council changed its stance?" Hope and disbelief characterize my question.

"Not yet, but as I told Allister, I will bring the matter before them as soon as I can," Lady A. promises. "Meanwhile, try not to take any undue risks. I feel like a confrontation will come sooner rather than later. You need not seek it out."

After letting her words sink in, Lady A. bids us farewell and disappears.

I sink onto the chair Lady A. recently vacated and look to Mistress Codee. The brief encounter with Lady A. has left me with a lingering sadness.

"I'm sure she will convey your regards to your special friend," says Mistress Codee. To my knowledge, she doesn't have the ability to read minds like Lady A., but her Gifts for Empathy, care, and support are unparalleled.

Pushing off the table, Mistress Codee gets up and bustles about the kitchen, starting water to make some tea and retrieving a pie from the refrigerator. In the short time I've been here, it's become an afternoon tradition for us. I protested at first, but I've come to realize that Mistress Codee has a Gift for service. As such, she genuinely enjoys fussing over me.

"Go ahead and see the images," says Mistress Codee. "The tea will be ready shortly. Do you have a preference today?"

I shake my head.

"Let's go with raspberry then. That will pair nicely with the pie."

I don't respond because I'm almost certain she's not really talking to me.

Today's pie is peach. While I'm eager to dive into the memory captures inside the capsule, I sense the routine putting Mistress Codee on steadier emotional ground. She's been exposing me to a different flavor of pie every few days. Since she never eats any, there's always plenty left over, so the neighbors benefit from her pie obsession as well.

Instead of picking up the memory capsule, I observe my caretaker. Mistress Codee can adjust her features to reflect an age range of about thirty-five up through seventy-five, but she prefers to be portrayed as a pleasantly plump mid-sixties, white-haired lady. She told me it suits her Pie Lady image best. As I wonder what she looked like as a teenager, I get an odd sense of familiarity and a fleeting image of a blond girl.

There's so much I don't know about Lady Elizabeth Codee. I'm struck with a sudden desire to hear her story. Everybody has a story. I wonder what emotions characterize her personal journey. Some life paths might not be as exciting as others, but given recent events, the idea of deep immersion in the mundane holds a lot of appeal. On the other hand, I could be guilty of judging based upon her current assignment of caring for me. For all I know, she could have come straight from the Spirit Plains Battle that has been raging for a few thousand years.

"Don't worry about me, lovey," says Mistress Codee, setting a mug of tea in front of me. "Eat up while the pie's fresh. If you'd like to watch the images while you eat, you can change the setting so it's not full immersion." She frowns. "It might be better that way."

Intrigued by her suggestion, I pick up the capsule and cup it in my hands, closing my eyes to concentrate. The device connects to my mind and asks what I'd like it to do. Instructing it to play the message in movie mode, I watch as the clear sphere flattens into an opaque, white screen and begins displaying its images.

The sequence isn't long, though it takes me a few seconds to adjust to the idea that these are Lady A.'s memories. They recount a brief encounter with a Despair demon. He changes shapes several times becoming Master Blaz and Lady A. before flipping to several others. Later, he stalks towards Allister while shifted to look like me. The joy at seeing my friend gets muted by his pained expression at seeing the demon imitate me.

I'm sorry.

Though I bear no guilt for the demon's actions, I wish I could comfort Allister. When I return my focus to the memory capsule, it continues, picking up from where I'd unconsciously paused it.

Lady A. sweeps Allister behind her, simultaneously shielding him and drawing her sword. A bright flash consumes the whole screen before it turns black and shows a still image of the first picture.

I stare down at it for three seconds, caught between hoping for more and wondering what happened. A spark of panic sails through me even though my logical side tells me that Allister must be fine. I feel bad about not immediately worrying about Lady A. and Master Blaz, but since Lady A. seemed healthy and she didn't say anything about Master Blaz, I assume he escaped the attack.

Setting the screen down, I look to Mistress Codee, whose gaze is fixed upon me.

"Why show this to me?" I ask.

"Adira thought you should know that the Prince of Darkness and his ilk have increased their mind games," Mistress Codee explains. "They are currently focused on young Allister, but they will do the same to you eventually. You must prepare yourself."

"How can one prepare to face such a thing?" I ask. "What did they do to him?"

"They threatened you, of course," she answers. "And Adira, Master Blaz, and Josiah." Her gaze becomes distant and pained at the mention of Master Josiah.

The first three make sense, but I can't find the connection to Master Josiah. As a Council of Light member, he's a valuable hostage for our enemies, but I'm not sure what his situation has to do with ours. When I ask Mistress Codee about this, she admits to not having an answer.

I finish the pie and wrap my hands around the tea, drawing comfort from the warmth.

Mistress Codee resumes her seat but says little, allowing me some thinking time. Her eyes fall shut either in prayer or mediation. She appears wearier than at the start of our conversation.

How will Lucifer and Hadeon come after us?

By focusing on my new duties, I've avoided dwelling on this issue. My assignment to a high school will protect me for a time, but I'm under no illusions the maelstrom of emotions will shield me forever. Part of my work will involve getting close enough to people to build trust, but I'm hesitant to place anyone in danger. Allister can handle trouble, and the demons targeting him aren't laid on my conscience.

"What troubles you?" inquires Mistress Codee.

"I'm supposed to protect people, not endanger them," I say. Unease does unpleasant things to my stomach.

"You are not responsible for humanity's problems," Mistress Codee assures me.

"I'm not talking—"

"Focus on the bigger picture." Her tone sharpens as she cuts in. "You caused neither the fall of mankind nor the rebellion in the Heavens. You are on Earth because the Glorious King has empowered you with the Gifts that can answer for a great evil and right something that went very wrong."

Physical fatigue gives me a headache. I groan and rest my head in my hands.

"These facts are not meant to add to your burden." Mistress Codee gets up and moves around the table to hug me.

The move forces me to drop my hands to my lap.

"I am merely saying that if the King believes in you, you have nothing to fear." Kneeling, Mistress Codee peers up at me and grips my hands. "If you can save someone, do so, but never accept responsibility for the actions of demons. They will carry forth their evil deeds elsewhere if not in our presence."

Warmth flows from Mistress Codee's hands. It's almost as hot as the tea mug when it was fresh. Her spirit reaches out to mine, but I keep my emotional shields intact.

"Let people in, Mina," she says. "You cannot protect them, if you don't love them."

Her words bring tears to my eyes. I fight to hold them in.

I do love them!

The protest shows up on my face. I'm not very good at hiding feelings in human form.

Mistress Codee's smile holds love and understanding.

"Don't fight those either," she advises. "They will cleanse your emotions and renew your soul. Just because you were asked to carry a burden does not mean you were meant to bear it alone."

The permission to cry breaks my emotional barriers. What starts as a steady stream soon changes to body-wracking sobs. Mistress Codee scoops me up like a small child and moves into the living room to the rocking chair. It creaks under our combined weight. My legs hang over the side, barely brushing the ground on the forward parts of the rocking motion.

Fluid leaks from my nose. I brush at it, trying to stem the tide before Mistress Codee's shirt is completely ruined. Embarrassment and shame settle in for only a fraction of a second before they're swept aside by Mistress Codee's spirit wrapping around me.

"You're still fighting," she scolds, once my sobs have subsided. "Being human is messy." She rocks a few more times before continuing. "I have spent a lot of time on Earth with people young, old, and every age and health status in between. They will tell you that outward beauty matters, but true beauty lies within and cannot be marred by tears."

After washing my face, I return to the living room where we have a long conversation covering many topics. Mistress Codee tells me stories of her recent work, including some amusing anecdotes from the animal shelter she volunteers at. She freely admits that she doesn't remember much from before one traumatic incident over a decade ago. I admire her ability to make peace with the pain of such a loss. By the end of our chat, she insists I address her informally. Of the options she suggests, Lady C. suits her best, so I shall call her by that name. Allister would tease me about mimicking him in this, but the gesture makes me feel closer to him.

Chapter 6:
The Sword Master's Apprentice

Case Report #: AK-117
Case Agent: Mistress Adira Clarimond
Guardian: Allister Knight

When I finally make it to the library, I expect to discover that I've completely missed the meeting. Instead, I find Aderes, Valin, and a third angel deep in discussion. They stop talking as I approach. Aderes sits up straighter and waves enthusiastically. Valin and the third angel nod politely.

They rise to greet me. Aderes looks especially tiny when compared to the tall, thin form of Valin and the large, muscular frame of the stranger. Most angels can modify their features and ages within a certain range. That range gets wider as our skill and experience increases, but most people gravitate toward a certain age instinctively. Aderes has chosen size and features suitable to a waiflike pre-teen girl with long brown hair a few shades lighter than mine. Her preferred weapon is a stubby dagger that suits her adorable human form. As my thoughts brush over her, warmth swells within me, echoing the pleasure of our Glorious King when he thinks of her. Aderes's Gifts center on encouragement.

There's a blue-white aura around Valin, indicating his strength and steadfastness. Even though we've barely exchanged a few dozen words ever, I feel like I know him. His devotion to the King is ardent, but somehow, I know it's only grown over time because of great trials he's faced.

I've always had good instincts about others, but this experience is on a whole new level.

As my attention fixes on the new guy, I get several impressions. First, a cool feeling tells me that he's keeping an emotional shield raised. Second, a pulsing yellow flash shows me the great pride he takes in his sword skills. Third, and finally, his dark skin practically pulses with a hot, white energy that tells me this is personal for him.

I frown, wondering when and where I picked up Empathy of this sort.

Aderes takes the lead with introductions, though I get the feeling it's only for my benefit. Jabir meets my gaze steadily. His black eyes hold both sorrow and fierce determination. He has short, dark hair covering his head and most of his face. Slowly, he holds out a hand for me to shake. We're certainly not bound by the current traditions of humans, but the handshake subtly informs me that he's aware of my newfound Gift and not offended that I'd read him instinctively.

"Master Josiah was my mentor at the Academy," says Jabir, as our hands meet. "I have returned to help find him."

He has a rich, deep voice that's pleasant to listen to, but I doubt he spends much time in idle chatter.

"Returned from where?" I ask. Our hands remain clasped because I'm not sure how to pull away gracefully.

"The Front," Jabir answers. He uses the physical contact between our hands to transfer images and impressions.

I get a glimpse of Master Josiah embroiled in an intense spiritual battle. He disappears, buried under an avalanche of demons appearing from nowhere. Panic grips me, but it's muted, like remembered pain. A sword flashes across my vision several times. Demons screech. Their chilling battle cries slice through me, but I ignore the burning pain, finally realizing this is a memory. The white emptiness changes into a green, rolling hill and then to the top of a mountain. Each new location offers the same sequence of complicated strikes, demon shrieks, and heart-wrenching glimpse of Master Josiah being overwhelmed and disappearing.

I mentally stagger under the influx of information. My body aches like I've been swinging a sword for days without rest.

Aderes moves through the table and grips my right arm to steady me.

"Try to relax," says Valin. "It's the quickest way to share what we've discussed thus far."

By the time I work out that the aches don't belong to me, Jabir has retrieved his hand, retreated a half-step, and folded his arms across his chest. He appears weary but content.

Aderes closes her eyes and lends me strength.

"I'm fine," I protest, trying to wrench my arm free of her grasp.

Anticipating this, Aderes releases my arm and places a hand on my back. Her hand is tiny, but there's no mistaking the strength she possesses. The touch is gentle and supportive, yet insistent.

"It'll go quicker if you stop fighting her," Valin notes. The blond angel has taken up a similar pose to Jabir.

They both watch Aderes work. It would be amusing if they didn't look so tense.

"Really, I'm—"

"Terrible at accepting aid," Aderes finishes. "We've each felt this and taken the time to recover properly. You don't have that luxury."

"Why?" I understand our mission is urgent, but surely, a few minutes of thorough explanation would be well-spent.

"A demon called Daeva has challenged you," says Jabir.

"Paige," Aderes supplies for my benefit. Deep sorrow marks her utterance of the name.

Something moves within my body and spirit. It's like two halves of me snapping together and accepting each other. I'm not sure what Aderes did, but she steps back with a satisfied look.

I'd known about Paige's threat of course, but this seems like something more specific.

"You needed my skills," Jabir explains, breaking into my thoughts.

I've always thought my swordsmanship skills were good to excellent, but the complicated moves I witnessed in that strangely real vision have the markings of master status work.

I get an upgrade? Cool!

The childish thought combats the weight of expectations

settling on my shoulders.

"What does she want from me?" I ask, referring to Paige's challenge. I don't care what she calls herself as a demon; she's still Paige to me.

"See for yourself," says Valin, "but first, guard your heart and mind."

At a gesture from Valin, an old-fashioned scroll appears in the center of us. From the grim expressions, I'm betting I'm the last to see this.

"The message will play if you let it," says Aderes.

I nod to the scroll, and it begins speaking with Paige's voice.

"Dearest Allister, you know how this will end. The only question is how many people—both humans and angels—you allow to suffer because of your stubbornness. Surrender to me immediately, and we can end this pointless war. I will wait a week for you in the desert. After that, I will hunt you down."

Anger crystalizes in my soul. The challenge is vague and unimaginative, but she's right to wait for me in the desert. We have unfinished business.

"Peace, Allister," says Aderes. "We're going to fight her."

"Together," adds Jabir.

I don't want to involve the others. Once Paige sees they're helping me, she'll attack them with every demon at her disposal. If our last battle was any indication, that's a considerable number.

"You need us."

Aderes's declaration sinks into my spirit.

"But we've never fought together." My protest isn't entirely true where Aderes is concerned, since we were part of a group that faced down a legion of demons infecting an old tree during our training.

"Doesn't matter," Valin says with a shrug. "We're connected through Jabir."

Jabir shakes his head once.

"We are connected through Allister," he corrects.

"You ... lost me," I admit.

"Your Empathy Gift from Lady Mina is very strong,"

Aderes says. She gestures to a large book sitting on the table they'd been working at. "I believe it's given you something called Transfer. That's—"

"The ability to temporarily allow Gifts to be shared," I finish.

Aderes beams.

I look at her sharply.

"You planted that thought," I say accusingly.

"I did!" she exclaims, "and it worked! Telepathy is a minor Gift of mine, but I'm still learning it. When I'm around you, it becomes a lot easier."

I give a neutral grunt and look to the other two.

"And what am I passively enhancing for you?" I ask them.

"Battle Meditation," says Valin. "I'm on crowd control and Aderes guard duty. She'll be directing you if needed."

"Swordsmanship," answers Jabir. "I will stand with you."

"But you're already a master," I say, confused.

"I am a Sword Master's Apprentice," says Jabir, "and anyway, even masters have much to learn."

"We're in a war. We need every advantage we can get." Valin looks at me impatiently. "Now, can we please get to the fighting?"

I can't argue with his logic.

"We're going now?" I'm not sure why I'm surprised. I guess I figured we'd strategize for a few hours before jumping into a battle.

"The conflict will likely end in a draw," says Jabir.

"But we need to show them we can't be intimidated," adds Aderes. "*You* need to show Paige that your fear and love for others lends you strength instead of crippling you as she wishes."

"If we know it's going to end in a draw, why are we fighting?" I ask. I'm looking for a deeper reason than Aderes's claim about showing Paige what we're made of.

"Think of it as a training exercise," Valin suggests. "One we cannot lose."

"This is also how we search for Master Josiah," says Aderes. "That's my job while you distract Paige."

I'm about to inquire further when I sense her silent

request for trust. Instead, I summon Tyre from the Veil. He lands in my hands. The others follow suit by drawing their preferred weapons. Aderes calls her dagger, Seassa. I never knew her dagger's name before, but it suits the little beauty well. Jabir's scimitar, Tommaso, appears in his hand and forms two identical swords, like mirror images splitting apart. Valin's spear, Asger, suits him. It's got a sharp end and a blunt end as all spears do. Delicate carvings cover every inch of the shaft and thin etchings decorate the blade. When Valin pauses to pray with the weapon, blue-with light pulses through the indented planes.

Tyre flares brighter in my hands, as if greeting the other weapons. He's never done that before.

"We are ready when you are," says Aderes.

I'd forgotten I'm the only one with Transporter and Teleportation abilities. The latter is a minor Gift for Valin and Jabir, but neither of them would be able to pinpoint the desert location where I first fought Paige. They couldn't carry Aderes there either since moving oneself through the dimensions and carrying a passenger involve two different skills.

Expanding my awareness to include my companions, I imagine an invisible capsule forming around us. Once we're tucked inside, I teleport the makeshift vehicle to the desert.

"Allister!" exclaims Paige, jumping to her feet. She'd been sitting under a scruffy tree with her legs crossed in a meditative pose. "You're sooner than expected. I've only been here an hour. I see you brought guests, but you're not exactly dressed for combat."

"I'm betting you brought company too," I say, though I can't sense any demons lurking about. I concede the point about dressing for battle, feeling stupid for neglecting that point.

Paige wears black leather armor that makes me think she's trying too hard to fit the whole servant-of-Satan thing.

My companions spread out next to me, Aderes and Valin to my left and Jabir to my right. We hold our weapons in hand but not quite in a threatening position.

"Of course, I brought help, but I wanted to discuss things with you civilly before things got messy," says Paige.

A spirit helmet settles into place around my head. I feel the rest of my armor set settling into place and glance over to see

Valin quietly praying. A moment later, armor encases Aderes too. Jabir has switched to comfortable pants, sturdy black boots, and a blue and white tunic. A turban appears on his head.

Paige shakes her head and claps mockingly.

"I'm impressed. Shall I tell my master you decline his invitation?"

"I never received an invitation," I say with a shrug, "but sure, I'm not feeling up for a visit yet anyway."

"Pity," Paige comments. She raises a hand and pockets of darkness begin forming above us like storm clouds. "I warned you others could suffer. Don't you care about dear Mina's health and safety?"

Despite the peace radiating from Aderes, the question bothers me.

"You can't trick me into revealing her location," I tell Paige. "I don't know it." I've never been so happy not to have a piece of information.

Paige laughs and snaps her fingers.

More demons appear.

"Then if you survive what comes, I advise you to find Mina and warn her about what awaits if she remains on Earth," she taunts.

"What's that?" I demand.

Paige looks concerned and compassionate now.

"We could give her a quick, painless death if she returns Spirit's Bane, but the longer she waits, the more she will have to endure. Can you have that on your conscience, Allister?"

Can you, Paige?

Chapter 7:
Dreamwalking

Case Report #: MN-118
Case Agents: Master Blaz and Mistress Codee
Guardian: Mina Nadir

Never thought I'd be much of a dreamwalker, but I'm distinctly aware of being asleep and witnessing events as they happen. It's terribly frustrating.

Allister, Valin, Aderes, and an angel I'm not familiar with face off against Paige and a generous host of demons. My connection to Allister allows me to know the new angel's name. He's by far the most skilled fighter, which makes me glad he's defending Allister.

Jabir fights with two curved swords. Every graceful swipe he makes slices through several demons. Most have chosen the form of small, simple creatures like bats or small birds, but others keep to their true, smoky forms. Still others got more creative with their earthly manifestations. Four demons combine to form a rampaging bull. Six chose to pair off and become wolves. Nine form nightmare creatures. These don't really exist but are great for terrifying humans. Some, like vampires, were inspired by human imagination.

I don't know how long the battle has raged, but Allister's expression contains anger and determination, which makes me guess not long. I confess to not seeing Allister fight with Tyre for several weeks, but his skills seem much more refined than I recall during our sparing matches.

Four nightmare demons shaped like gargoyles dive at Allister from above. I want to scream a warning to him, but I can do nothing. To my surprise, he finishes off his current opponent, a demon bird, and leaps straight up. When he's level with the gargoyle demons, Allister microjumps four times. Each move brings Tyre through one of the demons. They screech and turn to dust. Satisfaction surges through Allister, but a glance down at the battle wipes away the good feeling.

Two demons in human form have tackled Aderes and are dragging her over to Paige. Aderes's tiny dagger embeds itself in one demon's shoulder, but he merely yanks it out and tosses it away.

I focus on the dagger. Without truly being present in spirit form, I shouldn't be able to influence the dream, but I must try. Aderes cannot fall into Paige's hands. It would give her far too much control over Allister. Using the dagger as a focal point, I reach out with my spirit and cause Seassa to flare.

Allister flashes down to the dagger and picks it up, using both Seassa and Tyre to tear through the demons. He stands guard over Aderes as she heals the wounds dealt by the demons. A particularly deep gash in her left shoulder closes rapidly. I wasn't aware she had any healing abilities let alone skills of this magnitude.

Pain stabs through my chest, nearly waking me. The time in spirit form was less than a second, but Spirit's Bane noticed.

I'm going to lose the connection.

Allister's aura brightens then fades. Then, Aderes, Valin, and Jabir brighten for a split-second. A cut on Jabir's arm closes, finally cluing me into what's happening. Somehow, Allister is either lending the others his Gifts or enhancing their own.

Before I can dwell on which is the more likely scenario, a gesture from Paige halts the battle.

Jabir and Valin microjump to Allister's side. The three surround Aderes who has chosen to stay on her knees and pray.

"This is only a fraction of the force I can commit to the cause," Paige declares. "Why resist us?"

"Why hold back?" Allister counters. "Did your last failure destroy Old Lucifer's trust in you?"

"Quite the opposite," says Paige with a sickeningly sweet smile. "The amount of demons I could summon would crack the foundation of the ground we stand upon."

"You want a medal for that?" Allister fires the question with calculated disdain.

"Fortunately for you, my Master has asked me to be subtle … for now," says Paige, completely ignoring his question. "As I said before, the longer you—"

I never get to hear the end of Paige's speech as the chest pain awakens me from the nightmare. Clenching my eyes shut, I ride out the wave of stabbing discomfort.

Sensing my distress, Takoda whines and flops across my stomach. The movement tickles, forcing me to laugh, despite the fading pain. I catch him before he can prance up to my face and place him next to me on the bed. He yips in protest but settles into the new position by laying his head across my left shoulder. A wave of puppy breath hits me.

"You're lucky you're cute," I tell him.

He responds by licking my chin.

Sweat still covers my face and neck, but I hold him back so he can't give my face a thorough cleaning. Frustrated, he snorts and curls into a ball next to me.

Soon, he's snoring softly.

Joy and peace combat the dread filling me as I think over the fight. Paige's face comes to mind. Something about her smug attitude bothers me. Her smile looked like it held deadly secrets.

I concentrate on stroking the fur along Takoda's back and thank the Glorious King for the timely gift. Mistress Codee surprised me with him today. She volunteers at a local animal shelter three times a week. Normally, puppies get adopted almost immediately, but Takoda caught something called canine distemper. Since it's often a fatal disease, no family would consider him. The shelter director scheduled him for euthanasia. I'm not sure how Mistress Codee convinced Mr. Quigley to let her take him home, but she's very persuasive when she wants to be.

The viral disease was beyond Lady C.'s healing abilities, but she put in a request in the Prayer Room and the dispatcher sent someone to help her. Together, they restored the pup to full health. Apparently, once recovered, he spent the next few hours tearing through the house like a miniature wrecking ball.

When I returned from school, Lady C. kicked us both out of the house and into the backyard to play and get to know each other while she righted the house and puppy-proofed everything below knee height. She said I could name him, but at first, I had no idea how to do that. I've never had a pet before.

The idea of owning another living creature is foreign to me. Angels own materials and equipment that aid us in fulfilling our duties. We even bond with our spirit weapons. But our jobs as guardians, singers, or soldiers rarely leaves enough time on Earth to allow one to assume the responsibilities of rearing a pet.

I spent most of the first hour chasing the short black blur back and forth across the backyard. He paused often to sniff anything and everything. He chased squirrels, barked at the fish in the creek, and followed a bird in circles as it flitted around one of the four feeders Lady C. keeps in the tree near the kitchen window.

Upon Lady C.'s suggestion, I grabbed a few plastic bags, put the puppy on a harness leash, and took him on an official walk. Since the weather was sunny and unusually mild for this time of year, we met several people along the way. The two joggers ignored us, but the mother with two children stopped to greet us. Of course, everybody wanted to know his name. As I watched him bask in the attention and charm the family, his name came to me.

Takoda. I first heard of the word and its Native American origin in a history class during my month-long stay on Earth during my Academy days. It means *ally* or *everybody's friend*.

I need a friend right now.

The steady, rapid thumps of Takoda's heartbeats calm me enough to think.

It's good to see Allister in top fighting form, but the idea that Hadeon still has Paige pursuing him causes me to shiver, waking Takoda. He licks my face, whines softly, and snuggles closer.

"He's all right," I assure the puppy. "The others will protect him."

Doubt creeps in and sets up shop in my head.

45

It's only a matter of time before Allister falls into Hadeon's hands. If Paige fails, he'll send another. If that one fails, he'll send two more. And so on until he overwhelms my friend. But what then?

A vision of Allister wearing chains and kneeling in front of Hadeon strikes me.

I shake my head to dislodge the image, but it sticks with me.

What can I do to prevent such a thing from happening?

A gentle knock on my door breaks into my thoughts.

I blink at the door for two solid seconds before deciding to let Lady C. comfort me.

"Come in," I call, struggling to sit up without completely displacing poor Takoda.

Lady C. pushes the door open but stays in the threshold.

"Do you wish to talk?" she asks.

I shrug and scoop Takoda up to give Lady C. room to sit down if she wishes.

She perches in the middle of the bed and gives me a look that's part compassion and part evaluation.

"What should I do?" I ask. It's the same question that has plagued me for weeks now. "I want to help Allister, but I can't even help myself."

I don't really expect her to answer, but it's nice to have somebody listening who's present in the same room and able to hold a conversation.

"What did you see?" Lady C. asks.

Several minutes pass while I recount the dream and vision.

"Do you believe the vision will come to pass?" Lady C. inquires once I finish the tale.

I nod miserably.

Lady C.'s next words blindside me.

"Then, you are greatly blessed."

"I don't follow you," I admit, absently scratching the soft fur on top of Takoda's head.

"You've been given the chance to prepare yourself," Lady C. explains. "If that is the future, don't fight it, but do approach it with caution. The King never gives his servants a task

46

they cannot accomplish. The fact that you hold Spirit's Bane means our King believes you can conquer it."

"Does it frighten you?" I wonder. One hand wanders up to brush the large pendant's smooth surface.

"Of course," Lady C. replies. "It was never meant to be and could bring great harm upon many of our people. But if it was made, it can be unmade."

Her words echo those the King said to me when I first chose to keep Spirit's Bane. He added that the price had to be established and then paid.

What will you require of me? I silently ask the weapon.

I get the sense of something breathing curses in a language I'm unfamiliar with. That confuses me because human languages are accessible through the holy language. Since demons were once angels, I assumed they too spoke the holy language. That the object is speaking at all implies sentience, which changes everything about how I've been looking at this.

What are you?

This time, I don't get an answer.

"See, you've discovered something already," Lady C. says. She holds up a hand to stop me from explaining. "Keep the knowledge. If I know nothing, I can betray nothing."

Her words remind me of the dangers facing everybody connected to me. I'm humbled that anybody would accept the job of guarding me.

"There's nothing to know yet," I admit, "but there will be soon."

A glance at the clock tells me the night is quickly closing.

I need to spend some time thinking and praying though a plan, but I also have a job to continue in a few hours.

"Will you let me minister to you?" Lady C. asks.

Normally, I'd refuse because doing so will weaken her, but our many conversations are finally bearing fruit. A gift offered in love ought to be embraced.

Nodding, I gently pick Takoda up so he's not in her way.

Lady C. stands and sits next to me. She places her right arm across my shoulders like a cloak and lays her left hand on my forehead.

"Holy King, be praised through our lives and our works.

Flow through us. Give us grace to walk the path you've set before us. Every gift comes from your throne. You are our source of power. May we always have the wisdom to carry out your grand plan. The human body is frail but wonderfully made. Give Mina exactly what she needs when she needs it, be that strength or endurance or something else entirely."

Peace envelops me, pulling me down toward a deep, dreamless sleep. The last thing I'm aware of is Lady C. easing me onto the soft comforter and placing Takoda beside me.

Chapter 8:
Closing In

Dear Daeva,

I am pleased with your progress. Drawing Allister into another contest in the desert worked out well. I had my doubts the Council of Light would let him participate so easily. The part about using soul fragments as trackable links was ingenious. I anticipate that being very useful later, but do not act upon the knowledge yet.

The investigators have determined that Mina watched at least part of the spectacle as a dreamwalker. She is in New Jersey. It's the small, densely populated state below New York. That surprised me because I figured the Council would want her far from the Academy campus we clearly know about. Although there are about 3000 schools in the state, my people will narrow it down shortly. It makes the most sense to focus on the larger high schools since they probably hope to hide her presence behind the volatile emotions of teenagers.

I understand you're busy, and I trust you can accomplish your tasks without much oversight. However, I sense the Dark Master's patience thinning. I need details to share with him, so we will know how to best support your efforts and keep others from meddling. If I don't keep Than busy, he could become more of a nuisance for you.

You have several thousand demons who will answer your every order. And I am assigning you even more. You'll have close to three legions of demons and several dozen dark angels at your disposal. Use them. Always keep several demons with you, or at the very least, let them know of your plans. Regardless of which task you accept, there is a chance you will be forced to rely upon others. In such cases, it helps if there's already a measure of trust between the parties.

Speaking of tasks, do you wish to continue the pursuit of Allister? I ask because the opportunity may arise to ensnare Mina first and you have earned the right to help with that noble cause. Besides, their fates are linked. Capturing one is as good as snatching up both.

Revenge is a wonderful motivator, but only when tempered with calculation and caution. We cannot afford to reset Allister and release the Kindred Spirit Bond too early. Than's research indicates that such an event could cause Allister's Gifts to manifest in full in Mina. It is unlikely but possible that she could destroy Spirit's Bane if she harbored that much power.

There is a ritual that may help, but it requires the cooperation of at least one half of a Kindred Spirit Pair. According to the texts in the Grand Library, the bond can be voluntarily dissolved by either party. Regardless of which half you pursue, that is your primary objective. Convince one of them that destroying the Kindred Spirit Bond between them will allow the other to live in peace. Without the connection, Spirit's Bane will be able to finish Mina and you can give Allister a fitting end.

Give me your answer soon.

Hadeon, Servant of the Dark Master,

Director of Operations

***

Dear Lord Hadeon,

It's not my fault the Council never appointed a liaison for the girl. The two times it's been necessary, Lady

Clarimond has fulfilled the role herself. I believe I still have her trust, but she's not telling anybody where they're hiding the girl.

Now that we know which state to search, my demons will find her quickly. Give me your leave to capture her when they confirm the location. It doesn't make sense to put Daeva in charge of the operation. She doesn't know my operatives, and they won't answer to her.

I am aware she commands legions beyond the numbers I can boast but bringing that many demons into unfamiliar territory risks the delicate spiritual balance. I've worked very hard to keep this section of the country focused on their meaningless lives. We should not risk an awakening amongst the humans over this matter.

I would be happy to deliver the girl to Daeva once I have her. Should she not be working on a plan to control Allister anyway? Let me ease her burden and yours by doing this small thing.

Your humble and obedient servant,

Than

***

Dear Than,

Do not try my patience. I have no time for your petty jealousies, and if you interfere to the detriment of this mission, you will suffer.

We are closing in on our goal.

You may employ your demons to find the girl quickly, but do not approach her. Locating and capturing may seem one and the same, but they are not. There is a high chance someone must enter a school or a home to draw Mina out and subdue her. Most of your forces are ill-equipped for the infiltration side of that task.

Daeva prefers to work without the benefit of her legions. It's a flaw I shall address with her, but for now, I might be able to persuade her to work alongside you. Make no mistake. She's still in charge if the question of command structure arises. Do not take this as a slight. She has far more experience than you in this kind of work.

You both serve under me, and we collectively answer to the Dark Master. Any involvement in a mission of this level earns us glory, but only if we succeed.

Do not neglect your other duties. You have done excellent work in your region, yet there's more to be done. We cannot afford to grow complacent. I am hearing whispers of an awakening anyway. Find the leaders and neutralize them. Bring them personal tragedies, put them in pain, distract them, and otherwise remove spiritual matters from their minds by any means necessary. If you must kill them, do so, but that should be your last option. Destroying people by other means is always much more effective.

I have one other matter to discuss with you. The essence of Phobos must be retrieved. He sacrificed himself during the delivery of my message to Allister and the Council of Light. He was a good servant with excellent shapeshifting abilities. I hope to reset him, but I cannot do so while his soul remains bound to a crystal. I've assigned another agent the job of retrieving the essence from the Forbidden Knowledge Vaults, but he may reach out to you.

I am aware the undercover work wears upon you. The time for subtlety will end soon enough. For now, you are exactly where I need you.

Hadeon, Servant of the Dark Master,
Director of Operations

Part 2:
Pursuit

Chapter 9:
Fear and Fractures

Case Report #: AK-118
Case Agent: Mistress Adira Clarimond
Guardian: Allister Knight

The moment I'm back in the Heavens, I seek Lady A. out and show her the battle. We agree Paige held back but have no way of determining why. I'm sure it's because she did something that's going to come back to haunt us later, but not having the details is annoying.

As I stand to head toward my quarters, Lady A. stops me. The compassion and conflict in her expression warn me to brace for unpleasantness.

"The Council would like to see you, Allister," Lady A. says. The weight of her tone tells me to take the matter seriously.

"See me as in 'this is a formal summons' or 'this is a friendly invitation'?" I ask cautiously.

"Summons," she replies.

Two gentle raps at her door cause Lady A. to stiffen and speak faster.

"When you are before them, do not speak out of turn. Answer their questions as best you can, but do not volunteer answers to issues not yet raised."

I look at her curiously.

"Aren't you one of them?" I ask.

"Not in this matter," Lady A. answers. "I have elected to

be your advocate."

For what?

Thinking hard gets me nowhere.

Before she can further explain, the door to her office opens and two Council guards enter.

Lady A. stands and positions herself between us.

"I informed the Council we would appear, and so we will." Lady A.'s words have a sharp edge I'm not used to hearing from her.

"We are to escort you anyway," replies the nearest guard. He looks apologetic but not likely to back down.

Lady A. nods once.

"Very well, you may come with us, but you do not get to hinder him in any way."

"As you say, Lady Clarimond," says the same guard who spoke before. "He is your responsibility."

Facing me, Lady A. softens her tone but still speaks urgently.

"I'm going to teleport us to the Council's current meeting place. All members should be present, but don't be surprised if only one of them speaks. A trial like this isn't about you."

"What is it about?" I wonder.

"Transfer."

I barely hear her answer before her left hand brushes my shoulder.

A familiar split-second rush slams into my stomach, and we appear in a large, ornate chamber. The delicate work on the high ceiling looks like it took forever to create. Seven stone pedestals are arranged at even points around the circular room. Most have a Council member standing beside it, but the two behind and to my left stand empty. I assume those would have been occupied by Lady A. and Master Josiah.

Why am I on trial for Transfer?

Lady A. gestures for patience, turns, and stands a step in front of me while the two guards move to flanking positions.

Peering past Lady A., I'm dismayed to see Master Korin staring back at me coldly. He must be the Speaker for today's meeting. I don't remember much from my Council dynamics class, but I recall that sessions with a Speaker usually revolve around hotly contested topics.

"Today, we will decide the matter of Transfer." Master Korin directs the statement to his colleagues with his eyes. "We've heard testimony from the witnesses. All that remains is hearing from the source." His heavy gaze comes back to me. "When did you discover you had the ability to transfer Gifts?"

"A few hours ago." My tongue itches to say more, but a mental nudge from Lady A. warns me to keep my answers brief.

"Were you aware that practicing the Gift without the express consent of those around you is forbidden?" asks Master Korin.

"No, but I had permission," I answer. I think back to the library discussion. Technically, I'd probably boosted Aderes's telepathy before I knew I was doing it, but since she encouraged it, I assume she would grant permission. The other two were obviously aware since they told me what I'd be enhancing for them.

"So it would seem." Master Korin's frown does my soul good.

"The heart of that law is fear, and it needs to change," Lady A. declares.

"We know where you stand, Adira," says Master Korin. "The point of this session is to determine where Allister Knight stands and whether he poses a threat."

I bristle at his words.

"Of course, I pose a threat." The bitterness in those words well up inside me.

The Council members draw a collective breath and look like they want to draw weapons.

"To Satan and those who stand with him." I stare hard at Master Korin. "Why are we still standing around discussing things?"

"Careful. Your arrogance stems from pride," warns Master Korin.

And your reticence to exploit these Gifts stems from stupidity.

I mostly succeed in keeping that thought to myself, but a sideways glance from Lady A. tells me she heard it loud and clear. As it usually does, the use of big words reminds me of

Mina. I wish she knew how much I learned from her every day.

"And your fear stems from ignorance," I reply.

Master Korin looks like I slapped him.

"I'm sorry." I duck my head contritely. "That came out wrong."

"What did you mean?" Master Korin's tone could crack a foundation.

"I mean that the best way to combat fear is knowledge," I answer, keeping my eyes on the tiled floor. Over the course of a few seconds, a spirit of boldness comes upon me. I straighten and meet Master Korin's gaze. "If not much is known about Transfer, then let's expand our knowledge."

Murmurs of assent and disagreement come from the Council members around us.

I face each of them in turn before coming full circle to face Master Korin again.

"The Council of Light was formed to guide angels to reach their full potential," I remind them. "You don't know what I'm capable of because I don't know either. Help me find my way."

"Are you sure this is what you want, Allister?" Lady A. asks.

The sadness in her voice and the triumph in Master Korin's expression both shake my confidence.

"Maybe?" My inflection turns it into a question.

"Give us an answer," Master Korin demands.

"What's going on?" I direct the desperate question to my mentor.

"The Council wants to test and train you," Lady A. explains.

"Why do you make that sound like a bad thing?" I ask.

"The process could take several years," Lady A. answers, "and it would require little to no contact with the outside world, lest any of the experiments be tainted."

I immediately shake my head. I can't afford to make such a commitment.

"I take it back." I look to Master Korin. "Forget I said anything."

"Then, I hereby forbid you from practicing—"

"You don't have the authority to do that," Lady A. says, cutting Master Korin off. "You have to put it to a vote."

Master Korin's expression says he'd rather dip his toes in lava.

"Fine," he grumbles. "Let us each retire to ponder the matter."

Lady A. shakes her head.

"We've pondered enough. We need to act. Take the vote." She holds Master Korin's blazing hot gaze.

"You don't get a say in this," says Master Korin. He sighs. "But I suppose you are right." He clears his throat. "In the matter of Transfer remaining a forbidden Gift or not, how do you vote?"

"Abolish the law," says Master Blaz.

"Uphold the law," says Master Micah.

One by one the others vote. Master Titus echoes Master Blaz, and Master Korin does the same for Master Micah. Every eye falls upon Lady Deliah. She stares back at me with an unreadable expression.

"Abolish," she says at last.

"You're willing to toss a thousand years of precedent away?" Master Korin fires the incredulous question at Lady Deliah.

"The Gift hasn't manifested in a thousand years," Lady A. points out.

"And you're willing to let an untested angel run around using this unknown Gift?" demands Master Korin.

"Every Gift has the ability to be used responsibly and irresponsibly," says Master Blaz. "So, let's train him."

"He refused the training," Master Korin mutters.

"The old ways of training aren't practical," Master Blaz says dismissively.

"What are you proposing?" asks Lady Deliah.

Master Blaz shrugs.

"Mix in training days between missions. There's a lot to learn about Transfer, but it's only one of his Gifts. Let Allister continue his other duties while learning along the way."

The Council argues the point in several circles, but eventually, they agree to Master Blaz's plan.

Lady A. teleports me back to her office.

A few seconds of awkward silence pass.

"That was intense," I comment.

"That is an understatement," says Lady A., moving through her desk and sinking onto her chair.

"What would have happened if I'd agreed to Master Korin's training?" I ask.

"Let's be grateful you did not agree."

I press Lady A. for a better answer.

"We would likely take great losses for many years," she says.

"Why do you say that?"

"I don't need the ability to think forward to understand how the Council works, Allister," Lady A. says wearily. "Your word would have become your bond and my burden. You would become a prisoner in all but name. Meanwhile, the Prince of Darkness would find Mina. She would fight hard, but eventually fall."

"How do you know that?" My question sounds hoarse.

"Because the Kindred Spirit Bond can only prevail when the two halves work together. She needs you as much as you need her." Lady A. appears deep in thought.

I don't want to interrupt her thoughts, but I'm worn out from the tension. I need to rest my human body and renew my spirits. Perhaps a walk through the Tranquility Gardens near the Grand Library will do me some good.

"May I go now?" I ask.

"Yes, go get some rest," Lady A. says. "The Council may have vindicated you on account of using Transfer, but they still want you confined to the Heavens."

"For how long?" I try not to sound like a whiny child.

"Hopefully not too much longer but be patient. I will summon you when I have an answer for you."

Bowing, I exit Lady A.'s office.

Chapter 10:
Hold Nothing Back

Case Report #: MN-119
Case Agents: Master Blaz and Mistress Codee
Guardian: Mina Nadir

I can't do this anymore. For several weeks now, I've been trying to strike a balance between doing my job and hiding my presence from demons. The lack of commitment has gotten me nowhere. I know very little about anybody at school. I'm perfectly safe but also useless. Even the spiritual lifelines I established dried up almost immediately because I taught no one how to maintain them.

I can hide or I can be a guardian. Both simply isn't an option.

These thoughts run through my head as I stare at the middle set of glass double doors and prepare to enter.

Somebody slams into me from behind. The kid mumbles an apology even as he speed walks away. The brief contact tells me his name and a few of his fears. Keyon Jackson has a sore shoulder. He's resigned to failing the Geometry test today. He didn't do the assigned reading. He's afraid to ask Sheila Barr to hang out. And his parents' latest fight from two nights ago still weighs upon him. It had been bad. A lot of angry words had been exchanged. A chair got broken. Mom threw an empty liquor bottle at dad. Sidney—Keyon's older sister—threatened to call the cops but never actually followed through. Keyon had herded Alyiah and Teyar to the basement so they wouldn't witness the fight.

Might as well get to work.

Jogging, I catch up to Keyon.

"Are you doing all right?" I ask, stepping up beside him.

Keyon stops walking and stares down at me.

"Yeah." A dismissive tone hides the lie.

Reaching out, I catch his left hand.

"You seem down." I let go before he can pull away. The half-second of contact allows me to open my spirit to Keyon and silently encourage him.

You are loved unconditionally.

The words won't register with him, but the sentiment should. This time, I turn away. A faint burning sensation starts up in my chest directly below Spirit's Bane. Ignoring the pain, I'm a few dozen feet away before I hear Keyon's mumbled thanks.

I'm more subtle with the next few encounters. Each intervention causes mild pain, but I push past the discomfort. Since I'm not turning to spirit, Spirit's Bane should not be bothering me, but I suppose much of the work I'm doing requires spiritual Gifts.

It's getting closer to the start of school, so the hallways fill with a wide variety of students. After bolstering several more spirits, I slip into a doorway and concentrate on listening to several conversations. They're mostly a mixture of boasts and meaningless chatter until a trio of sophomores walk by. I recognize two of them from my social studies class and the third from gym class.

"You should tell someone!" hisses Samantha Ridgefield.

"It's not a big deal," replies Lilly O'Donnell.

"Do you still have the picture?" asks Brianna Sheldon.

I fall into step behind them.

"No! I deleted it!" Lilly's protest has too much force to be true.

"You didn't," says Samantha, calling her bluff.

"She didn't," Brianna agrees.

"Okay, so I thought about deleting it," Lilly admits.

Impatient, I quiet my spirit and reach out toward Lilly.

Having access to Allister's thinking forward ability carries the side benefit of occasionally being able to scan surface thoughts. It's barely more than what acute hearing would reveal if somebody mumbled a few sentences across an empty room. Although reasonably accurate from short distances, there are too many people around to get a clear handle on Lilly's thoughts.

Switching back to Empathy, I focus on Lilly. She's nervous, really wanting to impress Sam and Brie. Excitement and fear also mingle in her. The colors representing her emotions shift too rapidly to readily identify. By following the threads of her emotions, I gather that she's been texting with an older boy from Michigan. He recently sent her an inappropriate picture and asked for reciprocation.

Of the two girls with Lilly, Samantha seems most concerned, so I bolster her sense of boldness and fan the baby flames of protectiveness already forming in her. She should be able to convince Lilly to take the right steps to remain safe physically, mentally, and emotionally. Hopefully, the incident will foster a lasting friendship among the three girls.

The warning bell sounds, so I check my surroundings and head to physics class. I asked that my schedule be filled with more science than humanities classes since facts are much easier to replicate than opinions. I can already compose coherent essays, and I find it vexing to have to insert mistakes to emulate those around me. I'm aware that makes me sound like an insufferable twit, but I have already benefited from a thorough education in the Heavens in preparation for work on Earth.

The first class passes without much trouble. I minister to my classmates in subtle ways. We end up doing a lab exploring motion by firing a marble launcher and predicting where they will land. Since every other student in the physics class is a freshman, I expect more errant marble launches, but Mr. Chen keeps their attention with a smattering of leading questions and cryptic answers to their questions.

Each class, I finish the work and then request to take a walk. By now, most teachers understand I'm already comfortable with the material they're covering, so most of them grant the request. Since the classes run on a regular cycle, I can usually predict who will be on a walkabout at the same time.

Today, I meet Carlton Mahtur on his way back from the restroom. The minty scent surrounding him tells me he's probably been vaping. His mind is steeped in a haze of negativity courtesy of the songs he's blasting through his head nearly every minute.

I'm not sure how to help him.

He's perfectly content floating by as a practiced underachiever. The minor drug problem brings him a temporary thrill. Most of the excitement comes from the behavior being forbidden. If I get him busted, he'll get suspended. The administrators will likely split the sentence half in and half out of school. The in-school suspension will be boring for him, but it won't teach him much until his heart changes. The out of school time is a terrible idea because both of his parents work full-time jobs. He'll be home alone with his numerous vaping paraphernalia.

When he pauses by the fountain to drink, I reach out with my spirit.

You are better than this. Open your eyes and be free of the demons of self-doubt, self-loathing, and unworthiness.

To my surprise, a Sloth demon separates from Carlton. He freezes time.

I hesitate to engage him but remember my vow to hold nothing back. This time, I let a full shift to spirit happen. I'm back in human form an instant later, but the transformation was long enough to declare myself an angel.

"Move along. Move along," chants the Sloth demon. He takes the shape of a shadowy human and leans against some lockers.

A second demon emerges from Carlton. This one looks like a dull-eyed teenage girl.

My Empathy Gift allows me to identify the female demon as Apathy.

"This one is ours," says the Apathy demon. "Surely there are others worth fighting for."

"Every soul is worth fighting for," I reply.

"Call your spirit weapon and give us a good fight then," invites the Sloth demon. A new alertness enters his eyes. "Unless you can't."

"Who are you?" demands the Apathy demon.

"It's her!" The Sloth demon brightens with joy.

Panic tries to set in, but peace prevails. Stretching forth my hands, I speak with a voice of command.

"Be silent. Do not speak of me. You have no place here. Leave before I bind you in the name of the Glorious King."

I could do it, though I suspect Spirit's Bane would make me pay for such a move. However, I'm hoping they'll warn some other demons away. With baleful glances, the two demons bow and disappear. I second guess the wisdom of such a bold move. The command for silence will prevent them from running straight to Hadeon or Lucifer with news of me, but if I continue along a confrontational path, the stream of demons from this place will lead my enemies straight to me.

Fear nothing, dear child. The thought comes complete with the gentle, strong voice of the Glorious King.

Allowing time to return to normal, I slowly lower my arms. Carlton gives me a strange look and steps away, presumably headed back to class. I should get back as well.

My heart soars, encouraged by the words of my king, even as the stabbing pain encompasses my whole chest. Adhering to the time freeze must have required at least a partial shift to spirit form. I'm surprised the Sloth demon had the ability to manipulate time, and once again, I'm reminded that they possess many gifts like ordinary angels. Was the demon I encountered a recent convert? Could I have helped him if I chose a different approach?

The questions have no answers, but they do prompt me to pray for my enemies. War is messy.

The lunch bell rings as I make it back to class to pick up my backpack. Ms. Rollins gives me a disapproving look and reminds me to copy down the homework from the board. I do so before waving farewell.

Lunch becomes a prime time for reaching out to people since the vast majority of freshman through juniors pack into the cafeteria. The seniors race out to their cars to head home or to grab a quick lunch off campus, but every other grade is confined to the school grounds.

I stand in the long line to get a sandwich made to order

because it gives me a long time to minister to those around me. I've only met a few of these students. Gail Russman and Eddie Fisher have their arms wrapped around each other. Lust surrounds them. Though I sense several demons at work, I don't immediately drive them off. Instead, I pray for the two kids.

Lust cannot satisfy the cravings of your hearts. Your identities are not completed in each other. Get to know each other in heart and mind first. Let genuine love grow, not the superficial lies the world tells you is love. True love is patient, kind, and self-sacrificing.

When it comes to my turn, I order a plain roll. The woman behind the counter asks me if I'm sure I just want the roll three times before handing it over. Thanking her, I slide down to the register and pick up a jelly pack and a plastic knife before paying.

As I hand the register lady my money, she smiles brightly, but a sense of sadness and worry surrounds her. Reaching out, I pat her hand to get more information. Contact Empathy often proves more specific than stretching out with one's senses.

Rita Fuller's son, Todd, is out of work, depressed, and suicidal. I send a note to the Prayer Room for follow-up before sitting down to my simple meal.

The students at the far end stare for a short while before returning their attention to their phones.

As I eat, I wrap my emotions in a tight shield to take a short break and think back over the morning. I am proud of the work accomplished, but thereis so much more to do.

Chapter 11:
Could Be a Long Ride

Case Report #: AK-119
Case Agent: Mistress Adira Clarimond
Guardian: Allister Knight

A couple of boring weeks pass before Lady A.'s summons arrives. Before she can say anything, two quick breezes and faint pops alert me to the fact that we're not alone. Lady A. appears annoyed but not surprised. I glance over my shoulder and spot the two Council guards who escorted us up to the Transfer trial.

What now?

I spin to face the guards.

"They are not here for you, Allister," Lady A. assures me. She steps up beside me and addresses the guards. "Give me a moment to explain this to him, please."

They stare back at her stonily. The one who spoke the last time shakes his head slightly.

They're here for you?

The thought sears my brain as I register the fact that the other guard holds a set of spirit cuffs. I knew the Council of Light had some problems, but nothing could begin explaining a move like this.

"What did you do?" I sound dazed.

"Nothing yet," Lady A. replies. Her left hand lands on my right shoulder. "But several Council members would like that to

66

continue, and I cannot. You're needed on Earth."

Her words don't make much sense.

"I will deal with the Council in time, but we cannot afford to wait. Find Mina and help her destroy Spirit's Bane."

Lady A.'s charge barely brushes my ears before I'm standing in the middle of a highway.

A truck horn blares. Instinctively, I turn to spirit and attempt to revert back to my last location in the Heavens. The truck barrels through me, but since I'm fully spirit, its mass brushes past mine with a faint tingling sensation instead of sending me flying a few hundred feet. The angry horn blast trails off as the truck thunders past.

Disoriented, I take my human form and microjump into the woods next to the highway. Two more cars zip through the spot I just left.

Once my heart stops trying to bust out of my chest, I ease back into spirit and try the revert teleportation again. It fails. This time, I sense that Lady A.'s blocking me. Didn't know that was possible, but it's one more thing to add to a growing list.

Where am I?

The question triggers an answer within my mind: **Cold Spring, New York**. I remember the state from my last adventure on Earth. It's the same state where Mina and I finished our Academy training. My mood darkens. It's also where Mina got kidnapped. More cars whip past. Since night has fallen, I shouldn't be spotted, but I take a few steps into the woods anyway.

The sounds of moving vehicles fade, but not before I detect the familiar thrum of a motorcycle.

I take stock of the situation. Microjumping five times in a row disturbs much of the wildlife, causing a family of squirrels to yell and startling a deer. Punching a tree bloodies my right hand but confirms I can still heal. Once certain I'm far enough away from the highway, I summon Tyre. The Veil opens and lets him through without a hitch. More baffled than before, I let him return to the Veil.

Marking my current location so I can return to it, I teleport several times. My first jump takes me to Tokyo. I land on top of a large advertisement screen. The view is amazing but would be terrifying to experience in human form. The second jump takes me to somebody's basement in Kasimov, Russia. A third jump lands me in a large field near Sutherland, South Africa. It's a good thing I stayed in spirit form for these experiments because I stepped in something nasty in South Africa. Each time, I return to the highway near Cold Spring. Finally, I accept that my Teleportation Gift works fine on Earth.

Taking a deep breath, I attempt a jump to the Grand Library in the Heavens, but I'm not surprised when my surroundings don't change. I try my old Academy quarters. They would have reassigned the room, but I'm still familiar enough to find my way. That too fails.

"I'm stuck on Earth," I mutter.

I'm stuck on Earth!

The thought that echoes the words sends joy soaring through me. I've wanted to be here for weeks. It's not exactly how I imagined taking on a mission, but Lady A. made it clear I should find Mina and help her.

My mind starts attacking the first major problem: I don't know where they're hiding Mina. I consider opening my spirit to my friend. In theory, the Kindred Spirit Bond should allow me to track her. Sense stops me from taking the easy option. The Council hid her for a reason. Opening my spirit like that would also alert every demon on the East Coast and tell them where to find me.

The sound of a motorcycle again reaches my ears. This time, I think I hear my name being called. The sensation repeats several times. Curious, I ease to the edge of the woods.

"Allister! Allister. Come on, man. Don't leave me out here shoutin' at trees." The familiar voice wavers between pleading and demanding. A short distance up the highway, a man straddles a large motorcycle. The visor of his black helmet has been flipped up.

"Roy?" I call, solidifying my human form.

He turns so fast he nearly falls off the motorcycle. After catching his balance, Roy dismounts and yanks his helmet off. He jogs over but halts a few steps away, suddenly hesitant. Can't say I blame him. We didn't exactly part as best friends after he tried to turn me over to some demons. I didn't know his full name until his ma was scolding him when she picked us up from our last adventure. Roy Daniel Santori is about the last person I'd expect to run into after being unceremoniously kicked out of Lady A.'s office.

Hope she's okay. I push that thought aside and focus on Roy.

"What are you doing here?" I ask.

"I'm your ride outta the middle of nowhere," he answers. From his tone, I gather Roy is not exactly thrilled with the assignment.

"To where?" I wonder.

Roy answers with a shrug and a single word.

"South."

"How did you get the assignment?" I ask. "Who gave it to you?"

I want to ask him a dozen other questions, but I pause to let him get to the first two.

"Same as usual," Roy says. His accent gives the words a bouncing quality. "Got the impulse as I prayed. Told Ma I was going for a ride and started drivin'. Wound up along this stretch and felt I should call out to ya. You comin' with me or what?"

"How do I know you won't lead me into another trap?"

Roy looks at me like it's a dumb question.

"Ya don't," he replies. "But unless ya got a better plan, ya might as well stick with me." Turning his back to me, Roy walks back to his motorcycle and makes a show of donning his helmet. "The lady givin' directions tonight ain't much on details, but she seemed rather insistent I find ya these last few minutes."

"What lady? Is she still speaking to you?" I demand.

"Never met her," Roy admits, "but she sounds like a lady in my head." He blows out a breath and his shoulders slump. "Man, that sounds crazy." He shakes his head, sighs, and straightens. "Get on the bike if yer comin'. She didn't say nothin' about how far south we're goin'. Could be a long ride."

I think forward the possible scenarios. If I refuse the offer, I should probably head south anyway. The longer I stay in human form, the stronger the gut feeling gets. Mina is in that direction. I could cover the distance by microjumping, but there's no guarantee I'd find her any faster. I'd have to jump, orient myself, jump again, and so forth. If I accept Roy's help, at least I'll have someone to discuss ideas with. Can't say I fully trust him, but if he's an enemy, I should keep him in sight.

Roy unstraps a spare helmet and tosses it to me before climbing onto the motorcycle.

Since nobody's around and I've been meaning to test my microjumping abilities, I attempt to mount the bike using my Teleportation Gift. It works, but I land practically pasted to Roy's back, startling him. I quickly slide back on the seat and indulge in some cautious hope.

Worry for Lady A. presses upon me, but I decide to enjoy the ride for a while. Maybe it will help clear my head.

Predictably, trying not to think about the issue allows only thoughts of her plight to exist within me. I've no doubt Lady A. can take care of herself, but I got the impression she didn't want to physically fight the Council guards. The Council of Light must have forbidden her from sending me to Earth. Defying that order got her into trouble, but is it more than that? I feel like I missed something big and obvious.

More questions pop into my head as we speed south.

Why would the Council not want me on Earth? I know most members thought I should stay away from Mina, but is that the only reason? Why do they fear our reunion? Of course, the demons would love to get their grubby hands on both of us, but our chances of evading capture improve if we can fight together.

How can I find Master Josiah if I'm stuck on Earth? Instinct tells me the rescue mission to free him must happen soon.

If Lady A. blocked me from the Heavens, how long will it last and why would she do that in the first place? Hiding me from the Council makes some sense, but if they really want to find me, I can think of at least a dozen angels who could do so easily.

Chapter 12:
Carriers

Case Report #: MN-120
Case Agents: Master Blaz and Mistress Codee
Guardian: Mina Nadir

I finally met Kyrie Rostam. Though brief, our hallway encounter after lunch encouraged me as much as her. She has a lot of spiritual strength she doesn't even know about yet. I look forward to working with her.

Excited to tell Lady C. about my progress, I bound up the steps and burst through the front door. It's never locked since Lady C. likes letting the neighborhood children come and go as they please. Her specialty might be pies, but her cookie collection seems to be the main draw.

Coldness surrounds me.

As my smile disappears, I drop my bag and summon Kentaro. I turn my hands to spirit to hold the katana, but otherwise, I keep to my human body. At first, nothing seems amiss, aside from the unnatural chill. If I stretch the moment out, I won't have to face what comes. I pray silently and resist the urge to call out a challenge.

Give me wisdom and strength to face our enemies.

An orange kitten saunters in from the kitchen.

Where's Takoda?

Cute as the kitten may be, I doubt the puppy would

willingly relinquish control of the kitchen. The kitten stops a few paces from me and watches me curiously before licking a paw. A second kitten, this one black, dashes in and bowls over the orange one. Soon they're hissing, screeching, and scratching as they roll toward me.

I sidestep to let them pass. Three more cats occupy the threshold to the kitchen. A white Pomeranian sits primly behind them, and I begin to understand what has transpired. A line of cockroaches and spiders fans out behind the dog.

"Let the creatures go," I order. "They've gotten you past the defenses. There's no reason to torment them further."

The kittens have stopped fighting and taken to weaving in and out of my ankles. I back up a step and lower Kentaro to discourage them. They hiss at me.

"Do you not think me handsome in this form?" The sophisticated male voice emanates from the Pomeranian.

"The lifeforms on this planet are not your playthings," I say. "Do not be afraid to wear your true forms."

"We fear nothing," chorus the demons inhabiting the orange kitten near my left foot. She starts to cough. The fit turns increasingly violent.

"Come out of her!" I command, lowering Kentaro so the point hovers above the kitten's head.

Like a genie released from a bottle, a stream of demons exits the kitten. She staggers and collapses. I kneel beside her and gently stroke her soft fur.

Sleep, little one, they won't harm you now.

I lay a blessing upon the kitten. At least for a while, the demons will be discouraged from using her as a carrier.

Seeing what I've done, the black kitten yowls and leaps for my face. Solidifying my right hand, I catch him by the neck. At the same time, I plunge Kentaro through the kitten's body, releasing a flood of demons out his back. The black kitten mewls pitifully and goes limp in my hand. I set him down beside the orange kitten and bless him as well.

"I'm not going to ask again," I inform the demons. "I'm just going to keep stabbing."

Truthfully, I need to send Kentaro back soon. Spirit's Bane makes handling my sword painful.

The air above and around me thickens as the demons leave their animal carriers. I watch as the Pomeranian and one of the cats retreat, surrounded by the spiders and cockroaches. The two remaining cats dart forward, hackles raised and approach me slowly. I stand and back up so they won't feel threatened as they near the kittens. Each one picks up a tiny furball by the nape of its neck before wheeling and trotting out.

The demon horde melds into smoke that shifts back and forth across the ceiling above me. I eye them warily and hold Kentaro with my left hand only, leaving the right as flesh.

"Choose a speaker and state your demands," I say. I'm likely, not going to entertain them, but I need to know what happened to Lady C. and Takoda.

"Enter the living room and see for yourself." The voice is the same refined male voice that first spoke from the Pomeranian.

His excitement worries me.

A faint howl tells me Takoda's probably been confined to the backyard.

The demon cloud descends evenly on both sides of the room before parting like a curtain, giving me a clear passage into the living room, located to my left. With a sinking feeling, I step through.

My gaze sweeps over the room and slams to a halt on the rocking chair. It holds Lady C.'s slumbering form. A man wearing a black suit kneels before the chair with his left hand supporting her right arm. In other context, I'd think the scene showed a man sharing a tender moment with his mother, but nothing could be further from the truth.

I move Kentaro to a defensive position in front of me, well-aware how vulnerable I am with a demon horde behind and above me and someone much more dangerous before me.

The man pats Lady C.'s arm once before standing and turning toward me.

"Mina! So good to see you." Hadeon's greeting reaches out like a warm handshake. "There's no need for that." He nods to Kentaro. "Hopefully, we can avoid further violence today. Don't you think there's been enough suffering?" He waves to Lady C.'s still body.

She looks peaceful but a slight shimmer around her tells me I'm not really seeing her.

"What did you do to her?" I ask, trying to hold my voice steady. The hand holding Kentaro burns. I can concentrate on ignoring the pain or focus on the conversation. Knowing I'll need my full attention, I let my spirit sword slip back into the Veil.

Once I can concentrate, I gaze past the flimsy illusion. Lady C.'s face and arms bear dozens of red scratches. A deeper cut on her leg looks more serious.

"I got bored waiting for you," says Hadeon. He snaps his fingers and summons a dagger to hand. The tip is still bright red. "Had to be careful though, since she doesn't self-heal like you."

My anger spikes. I can tamp it down or embrace it. Choosing to let it work for me, I channel the anger into a flash of holy light. The demons around me shriek and flee. Hadeon shields his eyes but weathers the assault by staying in human form.

I suddenly realize he's not really Hadeon.

Though the illusion didn't waver, the spirit beneath did. Part of me traveled within the light. I've felt this spirit before, but I'm not sure where. He feels much younger than the real Hadeon.

"Who are you?" My question carries my irritation with it.

"I can be anyone," replies the figure. His features shift. In another moment, I'm staring at my own face.

"Cute trick," I mutter, "but my face doesn't suit you." I draw several ragged breaths, trying to recover from the exertion. Radiating that much light required a quick shift to spirit. Even though I'm back in human form, my entire being trembles with fatigue.

"Why didn't you say you wished for a private audience?" The demon, whoever he is, still mimics Hadeon's voice. His question has a light, teasing quality to it. He lets the dagger hover beside him while he adjusts his striped tie. "I could have arranged that without causing you such grief."

"Does your master know you're playing dress up?" I say. I need the demon to leave so I can tend to Lady C.'s wounds.

"Come with me." His invitation sounds completely innocent. "Both of my masters admire you greatly and do not wish to drag this out longer than necessary."

"Sorry, I'm not feeling sociable," I say.

Casually, the demon brings the dagger to Lady C.'s throat and looks back at me. "Tell me, how much do you value your caretaker?"

I try not to react because that's exactly what he wants, but my knees threaten to buckle. Frustrated tears sting my eyes. Thinking forward the problem doesn't help. If I surrender, the demon will likely kill Lady C.'s human form for spite. If I fight, she'll become collateral damage.

There must be another way.

There is.

It's not a great answer, but it's doable.

"A lot," I say, answering his earlier question.

While he processes my response, I microjump into him and switch to spirit form. Our cries collide as the light and dark briefly war against each other. Next second, I'm gripping the rocking chair arm hard to keep upright. The pain will crash on me soon, but I tap Allister's gift for manipulating time to delay it.

The demon slides back, but the contact between our spirits has revealed him.

"Time to go, Abdon." Dropping to my knees, I turn both hands to spirit and bless the ground. A pool of warm yellow light forms around the rocking chair, creating a small island.

"The more people you defend, the weaker you become," says Abdon.

"Love isn't a weakness," I reply, still suspending time.

"I look forward to proving you wrong," says Abdon with a slight bow. "It will keep the game interesting. Congratulations on saving one life. Would you like a hint as to my next move?" Before I can answer, he changes his face to reflect Aderes. "Remember, everything that happens to her is your fault. If you wish to spare her, surrender to any demon. They'll know how to find me." With a nod and a mocking smile, he disappears.

As soon as he's gone, the illusion surrounding Lady C. dissolves. The cuts around her neck are more serious than I thought at first. Her cheerful white and purple blouse has been marred by blood.

Finally letting my tears flow, I begin the healing process, dealing simultaneously with the deep gash on her left leg and the multitude of shallow slashes around her neck. I don't have to touch the wounds to heal them, since most of the work is done by spirit. Still, I need to feel the flesh knit itself together. I'm still holding time at bay, so I can work, but even so, Spirit's Bane causes a deep ache within my chest. Once the healing has completed, I let time move forward. The pain falls on me like a drenching rain, but I cling to Lady C.'s hand and fight for consciousness. By the time Lady C. opens her eyes, my entire chest feels like flaming arrows have pierced me.

"Thank you," she murmurs. A brief squeeze from her hand conveys her mixed feelings. She's grateful to be alive but filled with sorrow that it came at such a cost. "What did he want?" Her voice sounds hoarse.

"To deliver another threat," I answer. I quickly but briefly elaborate on the little I know about Abdon and his mission.

"You're not safe here," Lady C. says when I finish. She looks torn between calling down the armies of Heaven to defend me and telling me to run.

"Nobody around me is safe," I answer, gripping Lady C.'s hand fiercely. "Aderes has to be warned."

"I will handle that part." Lady C. closes her eyes and switches to spirit form. Her human form will need time to recover from the trauma even though the wounds are gone. "You must go to the secondary safehouse."

"I need to see some people," I counter. I jump to my feet and sway until my head rights itself. Everybody I've worked with today will be marked by the experience. If I'm right, that means the demons could use the connection to track them down.

"No, you need to stay free," Lady C. says quietly but firmly. "I will have the Prayer Room send help for your charges but remember that the demons have little direct power over humans. *You* are the prize they're after."

And Allister.

I should reach out to my friend. He would know how to lift my spirits, but I'd rather face Hadeon and Lucifer alone than have Allister suffer too.

Chapter 13:
Low Profile

Case Report #: AK-120
Case Agent: Mistress Adira Clarimond
Guardian: Allister Knight

By the time Roy pulls over in a diner parking lot, my legs feel molded to the seat. I dismount carefully, tempted to change to spirit. Instead, I stretch my legs and back, hearing a series of satisfying pops.

Roy gives me a quizzical look.

"Do angels get hungry?" he asks.

"If we stay in human form," I answer. My stomach agrees with a gurgling noise.

His gaze flicks from me over to the diner and back. Then, he sighs.

"Don't suppose y'all carry cash or credit cards," he comments.

I shake my head, grateful Lady A. thought to send me a guide in this strange place.

"I can get cash if I need to," I assure him.

Technically, I've never met The Trader, but Mina has. He's in charge of making sure monetary gifts get where they need to go in the Western Hemisphere. Most gifts are meant to be delivered to humans, but angels on long-term assignment have such needs too. Since my mission isn't exactly Council sanctioned, I'm not sure I want to test my luck.

"Nah, no worries," says Roy. He starts walking toward the door. "I can spring for a meal this time." Reaching the door first, he swings it open and ushers me in. "Won't make us square, but maybe it'll do some good."

I consider telling him that's not the way forgiveness works, but Roy moves past me and pulls open an inner door. Music and movement hit my senses simultaneously. A young man lugging a bin full of dirty dishes deftly dodges around a woman supporting a heavy tray. She glares at him but continues along her way. A different man straightens after delivering a round of drinks. He smiles and says something to his customers before stepping back directly into the woman's path.

Freezing time, I position myself behind the woman. Next, I allow time to proceed at half-speed. The male server bumps into the woman, sending her tray flying. I catch the tray as it slips from her grasp and steady her with my other hand.

As time resumes at normal speed, a round of applause and whistles rise from the three nearby tables.

"That was awesome!" shouts a boy. "You're like Spiderman!"

A toddler sitting next to the boy stares up at me with wide eyes. Drool drips down his chin before his mother reaches over and swipes at it with a napkin.

Ducking my head, I hand the server lady back her tray. She thanks me and hurries to make her deliveries. Shoving my hands into my pockets, I shuffle back over to Roy.

A brief headshake conveys his disapproval, and he keeps his lips set in a firm line as we wait. I'm not sure what we're waiting for until a young woman steps up and asks us to follow her. Soon, we're seated in a booth well away from the front door. I slide into the long seat and take in my surroundings. Don't think I've ever sat on anything quite so red before. The table gleams and the ad-filled paper placemat sticks to some damp spots. The faint scent of lemon lingers over the booth.

"Quit starin' around like you ain't never seen a diner before," Roy says in a low voice.

"I haven't," I admit.

"You wanna stare at somethin', look at this." Roy shoves a large booklet into my hands.

"What is it?" The question earns a dumbfounded look from Roy before he realizes I'm messing with him. I've seen menus before. We had a few classes on interactions with humans. The sample menus were quite a bit smaller than this one, but I get the general premise.

The woman I caught a tray for bustles over and drops off two glasses of water and a few straws. She introduces herself as Meredith and promises to return for our orders shortly.

I flip through the entire menu. Everything sounds intriguing, though the descriptions and the names don't often line up. I rule out 80% of the items based on their meat content. We're not forbidden from eating meat, but I've never gone out of my way to get it. Turning to the front again, I start over, scanning slower this time.

"Need a recommendation?" Roy asks tentatively.

"What are you having?" I ask, instead of answering.

"I'm thinking the 'Meat Lover's Biggie Breakfast'" says Roy.

I check it out. The meal comes with three eggs served to order, three strips of bacon, three sausage links, and a slice of scrapple.

"What's scrapple?" The name doesn't make it sound that appealing.

Roy's grin has an evil glint.

"Best not to ask what's in it," he advises.

Meredith returns while we debate the finer points of knowing something versus being blissfully ignorant. Roy follows through with his meat lover's order and asks for coffee. I stick with the water and choose something called penne vodka without the added meat option.

"That comes with soup or a salad, love. Which will it be?" asks Meredith.

She rattles off a choice of five different soups. Overwhelmed, I choose the salad without any dressing. That earns a raised eyebrow from Meredith, but she snaps up the menus and tells us she'll be back with the salad soon.

Roy fiddles with his straw wrapper. I can tell he's brimming with questions, but I decide to see how long it'll take him to get around to asking them. My eyes wander over to the many colorful items sitting on our table. There's salt, sugar, pepper, ketchup, and short, stubby writing implements with waxy coverings. I pick one up.

"They're called crayons. Kids use 'em to draw on the placemats," says Roy. Once again, his voice dips low during his explanation.

The placemat seems plenty full already until Roy grasps the corner of his and flips it up to show me the underside.

Curious, I sweep aside my fork, knife, and napkin and turn the placemat over. The back looks like somebody tried to sketch half the animal kingdom. A baby tiger stares up at me with big, friendly eyes. Before I can test the yellow crayon, Meredith drops off my salad. I absently thank her and move the salad aside.

Roy snatches the writing thing away.

"Try to act normal!" he hisses, chucking the crayon back toward the others sitting near the sugar packets. "Teenagers don't do crayons unless it's to draw somethin' obscene. Eat yer salad."

"I didn't know you cared, Roy," I say, struggling not to smile. Picking up a piece of lettuce, I munch on it while giving silent thanks for the food.

"Use a fork!" Roy scolds.

Chuckling, I let manners take over and eat the salad with proper utensils.

"Why do you care that we blend in?" I ask.

"Why *don't* you care?" he fires back. "This place could be crawlin' with demons. I wouldn't know the difference if they're inside people, but I do *not* want to draw their attention tonight."

He makes a good point. Bowing my head, I close my eyes to concentrate and reach out to see if I can sense any demons. Getting nothing, I send out subtle waves from my spirit. They won't do much, but the move might trick some demons into revealing themselves. Grabbing my water glass, I take a few sips and scan the room slowly. Instead of looking with my human eyes only, I tap into my spirit eyes to see if it worked. The effect is similar to a human with The Sight.

Three Sloth demons surround a table of men wearing business suits. A little Chaos demon scrambles from table to table whispering to the small children. A Despair demon shadows some of the servers. For a place this size, that's a reasonable number of demons to be working at one time. They probably came in with the people they're hovering near. I stop looking with spirit eyes and report to Roy, even though his grim expression tells me he's aware of them.

"Don't think they're concerned with us," I conclude.

"Good. Let's keep it that way," he says.

Meredith appears with our food. As she walks away, I notice the dip in her shoulders. Unable to resist, I peek into the spirit realm again. Sure enough, the Despair demon has hitched a ride on her. He's in the form of a cute, harmless teddy bear.

Sensing my attention, he twists around and bares his teeth at me. His paws remain pressed into Meredith's back.

"Excuse me, this won't take long," I say, pushing up from my seat.

"No. No. No!" Roy chants. "Whatever it is just no!"

Once again halting time, I summon Tyre and microjump to Meredith's side. I wait a couple of seconds for the demon to shrug off the effects of the time freeze and point Tyre in his face.

"Find somebody else," I say.

"Why?" demands the little Despair demon. "I founds her first. *You* finds somebody else!"

A quick check reveals no seal on Meredith. She's unclaimed. This could get tricky. I'll have to try reasoning with the demon. Things are always easier when there's a holy seal. Where's Mina when I need her? She's much better with words.

"Look, it's been a long day," I begin. "She's my server. I'm trying to look out for my own. You've got a job to do, and I get that. I'm just asking you to do that job elsewhere."

"You is a strange angel," says the Despair demon. He conjures a little black card. At first, it looks blank, but there's a thin gold circle in the center. "You ever wants to switch sides, press thumb to center circle. We helps you." With an ear-piercing cackle, the Despair demon retracts the tendrils he'd planted in Meredith, leaps onto a table, and skips through a window.

I microjump back to my booth and release my grip on time.

Roy's pale face has deep red streaks running through his

neck and cheeks. He's gripping his fork like he'd enjoy stabbing me with it.

"Do I wanna know what went down?" he wonders.

"I got a souvenir," I say, waving the small black card. I tuck it away in my back pocket. "This smells great."

It's a graceless transition, but Roy lets it slide.

We spend the next few minutes in semi-awkward silence, shoveling food into our faces. By the time I maneuver the last noodle into my mouth, I'm full. Roy uses the last of his crust to scrape up some of the egg on his plate and tucks it away.

"Wow, you boys must have been hungry," says Meredith. There's a new brightness in her eyes. "Can I get you anything else?"

"The check, please," Roy answers.

When she's gone, he studies me.

"You're really lousy at this low-profile thing," he notes.

"I like helping people," I say. "What's wrong with that?"

Roy looks up like the ceiling will offer him some grand inspiration.

"Look, Al—" Roy cuts himself off and leans close, whispering again. "This ain't even like the last search for yer friend, man. And that one felt heavy. This is much bigger."

"How do you know?" I'm curious to know what Roy's feelings stem from. I believe him, but I've never heard of a gut-feeling gift without a specific name.

Roy glares.

"How many times I gotta say I don't know—"

"Here we are," Meredith interrupts cheerfully. "Take your time with that. It's been a pleasure to serve you." Without being asked, she tops off Roy's coffee and rushes off to another table.

After a few deep breaths, Roy starts again.

"If I pray, I sometimes hear from ang-uh yer people." He takes a long swallow of coffee and winces as it scalds his mouth.

Reaching out, I touch his cheek and restore the damage.

He mumbles thanks before slapping my hand away.

"Anyways, sometimes I hear words and sometimes I get feelin's." Roy stares into my eyes. "The one I got now ain't pretty."

"What's it saying?" I ask, not quite ready to believe his

premonition.

"We gotta hurry. Something bad went down today." Roy grabs my hand to keep me in place and hurries on. "I don't know anything else, but ridin' at random on my motorcycle's not gonna work. I hope there's a backup plan."

Chapter 14:
Flight Plan

Case Report #: MN-121
Case Agents: Master Blaz and Mistress Codee
Guardian: Mina Nadir

The secondary safehouse is on an abandoned farm in Clarke County, Iowa. The easiest way to get there would be to teleport, but I've never used Allister's Gift to travel that far before. In theory, Teleportation shouldn't be affected by distance, but I can't afford to get this wrong if Spirit's Bane fights me mid-jump. I'm more comfortable with microjumping but traveling such a distance would take a long time.

Spirit flashing is another option. It's how most angels move from place to place on Earth since Teleportation is a relatively rare Gift. It never seemed rare at the Academy because most of the faculty possesses the Gift. I don't know how quickly spirit flashing allows one to move in human terms, but the guest lecturer said it was several times faster than current jet engines. As with Teleportation, one needs a very specific destination in mind to avoid being many miles off target.

Reena gave me two cards with coordinates when she dropped me off at Lady C.'s place, but I'd hoped to never need them. Idly, I finger the card she said to use first. This one will let me know where to find the farm.

Lady C. watches from the doorway to my room with a softly whining Takoda in her arms. I've already said my goodbyes. Only the actual leaving part remains.

Teleportation or spirit flash?

True teleportation sounds risky. Microjumping and spirit flashing are similar in terms of the end results. Only the means differ. Microjumping is considered teleportation because one disappears from their current location and appears elsewhere. Usually the destination of a microjump happens to be within twenty meters of the origin point. Spirit flash, on the other hand, involves one moving through every inch of space between the origin and end point. That would be the best option, except for Spirit's Bane. I'm not sure I can stand being fully spirit for the necessary amount of time.

Do both.

The answer seems obvious. If I can plot a reasonable course from here to the Iowa farm, I should be able to spirit flash to each city or town along the way. In theory, the plan would let me get there quickly without taking my spirit form for more than a few seconds at a time. I'll have to access the universal knowledge or run a few internet searches to plan appropriately. Both are trackable, but if I keep my queries general, I should be safe enough. Nothing dictates that I must travel in a straight line anyway. If I move continually west, I should be fine.

I hate running, but since I've not settled on a way to destroy Spirit's Bane, I'd rather it not fall into Hadeon's hands.

To start, I walk out of the room, stopping to give Takoda and Lady C. one more hug.

"Your bag is by the door," Lady C. reminds me. "I packed you two sets of clothes and some food. There's also almost two hundred dollars in cash but use it sparingly. I don't know when your next contact will find you."

Takoda yips and lunges for my left hand as it passes. He misses and sinks his teeth down into my Hill Crest Comets sweatshirt, ripping the fabric.

"Maybe you shouldn't wear that," Lady C. comments. Her frown tells me she's not simply referring to the sweatshirt being damaged.

I'm not sure how closely Abdon paid attention when he was here, but I should not take anything that ties me back to this town.

"Always looking out for me," I murmur. After freeing the frayed end from Takoda's fierce grip, I plant a quick kiss on the top of his head and cup his soft face with my palm.

I'm really bad at this fugitive thing.

I nod to acknowledge Lady C.'s concern and slide past her back into my room. Soon, I'm wearing a light blue sweatshirt with a yellow smiley face on it. Carefully, I fold the Hill Crest sweatshirt and lay it in the center of the bed.

The trek down the stairs feels painfully long, but I make it. Takoda howls from the top of the stairs. Lady C. tries to comfort him. I don't dare look at either of them. Instead, I pick up the waiting backpack and exit through the front door.

My first stop is New York City. I spirit flash to one of the tunnels under Pennsylvania Station where people get on and off trains entering from New Jersey. Since the one I chose was empty, I microjump over to a different track where people are still trickling off a recent arrival and trekking over to the escalators up. A conductor does a doubletake but shrugs as I jog past him. The two short stints in spirit form cause some pain, but I ignore it, since it's relatively mild.

Since the train station attracts a lot of humans at all hours of the day and night, it's naturally a hub for angels and demons as well. Peach and pink lined hallways greet me as I enter the main floor. A disheveled man with a desperate look watches me. I peer into the spirit realm to make sure he's not demon possessed. He's not, though several Mockers call out hateful things to him. I wait for several blurs to speed by me, letting me know other angels are passing through before initiating my next spirit flash to Grand Central Station about eight blocks up and a few avenues over toward the East River.

I hadn't planned on going there, but it gave me an excuse to move through the Mocker demons. They scatter and tumble like leaves caught in a hurricane. My stay in Grand Central Station is no longer than the one in Pennsylvania Station, but both stops allow me to absorb the universal knowledge of a wide variety of travelers. I'll need some time to process the information, but I'd rather do that at a quieter location.

I spirit flash to each of the local airports. This grants me a different kind of knowledge, since pilots and flight attendants tend to travel regular routes.

My next stop after LaGuardia airport is the Amtrak station on 30ᵗʰ Street in Philadelphia, Pennsylvania. It occurs to me that humans reuse names quite a bit. I started my journey in a train station bearing the name Pennsylvania and spirit flashed almost a hundred miles from New York City to an entirely different state, only to end up in a place called Pennsylvania again.

Also, that hurt like somebody poured a strong acid on my neck. I received the mental comparison from a chemistry professor who works at Columbia University in New York. He accidentally touched a bit of high concentration sulfuric acid while in grad school. I have the advantage of being able to heal any significant damage Spirit's Bane inflicts on my body, but the necessary shift over to spirit to heal also takes a toll.

One thing's certain: I need to keep the spirit flash episodes a lot shorter than a hundred miles.

Needing a quiet place to think, I walk over to the Drexel University campus. My wanderings take me to a line of benches near the Korman Center. Exhausted, I sink onto a bench and close my eyes. Processing goes slower than usual because I need to keep alert for trouble.

The only close call happens when a campus security guard stops on one of his rounds.

"Are you all right?" asks the guard.

"Yes, of course," I answer. Not wishing to lie to the man, I microjump to the far side of the building. He'll have a nagging feeling for a few hours, but then forget the encounter altogether.

The late hour doesn't give me much of an excuse for staying outside, so I tap into the knowledge around me until I find a young woman who uses the 24-hour study space in the Queen Lane Library a lot. Most of those would require a reservation, but every library has little corners one can disappear into for a few hours. Finding one such corner, I eat a power bar Lady C. packed for me and take a nap, using the backpack for a pillow. More specifically, I take a series of ten-to-twenty-minute naps, each time waking long enough to move to a new location farther away from people.

As the night melts into a new day, the number of people

in the library increases drastically. I find a desk and consider my next step. I could cross the three hundred-some miles directly to Pittsburgh, but that's a very long spirit flash.

Maybe I should try teleporting. It'll be a lot easier than trying to plot a random path through the rest of this giant state. Most cities and towns bunch near the major highways. Routes 76, 78, and 80 are all options, but I'm not even certain I should travel near populated places. They afford a measure of anonymity, but more people means a higher chance of running into demons.

Most problems have simple answers. The thought comes complete with Master Blaz's voiceprint.

Although I'm eager to get to the safehouse, there's no timetable. If I take a train, I can stay in human form and rest my body. Digging through the backpack reveals the cash Lady C. mentioned. It amounts to $195.00. A quick survey of the minds around me tells me I can buy a ticket at the station, but it'll be more expensive than if I order online. I won't need a return ticket, so it should be fine. Since the next train doesn't leave until 9:20 a.m., I have enough time to walk to the station. I need the exercise, plus I'd rather not keep microjumping. Each use of that Gift increases the chances of detection.

I make it back to the Amtrak station with enough time to buy some orange juice and a bagel for breakfast. After purchasing my ticket, which consumes more than half the money I have left, I sit down to eat. The need to continually sustain a human body takes time and effort, but I'm starting to get used to the rhythms.

I try to resist the urge to people watch in both the natural and spirit planes, but I can't help it. Either my training was too thorough or I'm just nosy. Many people buzz with the excitement of a new adventure, telling me they're probably going on vacation. Quite a few others have a neutral attitude that marks them as regular commuters. Curious, I examine the feelings of one man more closely. A train seems like a difficult means of travel for a regular commute. It doesn't take long to discover his very strong, irrational fear of flying. Even now, he's terrified of what could happen to the train.

There's no Anxiety demon hanging around him, so I conclude the fear stems from elsewhere. I check to make sure the spirit presences are paying little to no attention to me. Then, I reach out and wrap the man in a silent blessing, replacing some of the fear with peace. He won't dash to an airport to hop on a plane, but it should remove some of the tension from his shoulders. The effort leaves me tired since I didn't exactly get a great night's rest.

I don't like having these energy limitations.

Leaning my head back against the wall, I plot ways to rid the universe of Spirit's Bane.

Since it's a spirit weapon, there should be a supernatural answer. But its influence upon my physical form has been increasing. That means it's adapting. I'm starting to think it has a mind of its own. Perhaps that means there might one day be a physical solution to the problem.

Blaz's advice runs through my head again.

I repeat it silently, almost like a mantra.

Simple solution, simple answer.

The seed of an idea begins to form.

Chapter 15:
Predecessor

Case Report #: AK-121
Case Agent: Mistress Adira Clarimond
Guardian: Allister Knight

Since I never had a plan, there's certainly no backup plan. Needing a moment to think without Roy's nervous energy buzzing near my head, I duck into the restroom and throw some water on my face. He comes in behind me and heads toward one of the stalls. I could dispense with the need to answer my human body's natural rhythms by flipping to spirit even for a second, but I choose the route less likely to freak Roy out and avail myself of the open stall.

"What are we gonna do?" Roy asks when we meet up again by the sinks. He keeps his voice low even though we're alone in the restroom. After washing his hands, Roy lets the water run while he waits for my answer.

"Take a ride," I reply. I too wash up and throw more water on my face. "I'll let you know when we're on the road."

I can feel Mina's nowhere near us, but a sense of her lingers. If I'm careful, I can probably locate where she's been. The safehouse should have measures to prevent most means of tracking somebody, but the Kindred Spirit Bond gives me the advantage. I'm torn between following her and starting from the beginning. A vague west-of-me feeling is all I currently have to go on. If my mental map of the country's correct, east-of-me would be the Atlantic Ocean. Needing more details, I decide to find the safehouse first.

As we did during the first search for Mina, I direct Roy through subtle signals and brief instructions through the closed communications system he had installed in the motorcycle helmets. We start out in the wrong direction, but I quickly sort the feelings and point Roy in the correct direction. Within twenty minutes, we're pulling up in front of a small but peaceful looking gray house at the end of a cul-de-sac.

Roy dismounts, pulls off his helmet, and looks at me expectantly.

"You gonna check it out or keep starin'?" he asks.

"Are you getting anything specific?" I ask, also removing my helmet.

"Nah, but that gut bad feelin' is kickin' in somethin' fierce," says Roy. "I think I was wrong about whatever happened being over."

Microjumping off the motorcycle, I turn to spirit and summon Tyre.

"Stay here," I say.

"You must be outta yer head," Roy mutters. "Stayin' here is a one-way ticket to the slammer. Jus' take the lead, will ya?"

He has a point. The neighborhood looks like the type to call the cops for a messy flowerbed let alone a burly guy loitering in a driveway next to his motorized behemoth, especially when he appears to be chatting with the air. Roy has The Sight, so he can see me fine in spirit form. The other 99% of humanity isn't so lucky.

Though tempted to microjump into the house, I want to stay close enough to Roy to protect him. Letting my spirit sword lead the way, I slowly approach the front door. Roy knocks for us. The sound sets a dog to barking. A female voice says something to the dog. The barking subsides to low rumbles, then stops. I'm suddenly not sure what to do with Tyre. Keeping him in front of me is the sensible thing to do, but it's a tad aggressive, seeing as I'd like this lady's help. I settle for a two-handed resting pose.

The door swings open, giving us a good view of a slipper-clad, bathrobe wearing woman in her mid-sixties. About the only thing that could make her look more harmless is the little pink curlers that went out of style decades ago. A huge smile lights up her face, making me wary.

Tyre's up and at her throat in an instant.

She chuckles. Not only does the voice not match, but it sets my teeth on edge.

"Come in, Allister," says Paige, turning her back on me.

"Give me one reason not to skewer you." I barely keep the words at a normal volume.

"Because you won't get your answers," Paige replies, turning around to face me. Thankfully, she returns her features to normal. She's now wearing jeans and a loose, flower print blouse. A small section of hair on the left side of her head has been braided and held back by a clip. The change enhances the youthful innocence she projects. The blond teenage girl act suits Paige better. It also makes me feel slightly less guilty about wanting to punch her.

"Never thought I'd see that," says Roy.

I stare at him and flick my gaze over to the motorcycle. I should jump him to safety.

He shakes his head.

I don't have time to argue with him, but I'm still not ready to step foot into Paige's quaint trap.

"Invite your friend in too," Paige says. She gestures and a dark cloud starts drifting away from the door toward the kitchen.

A growl escapes the cloud.

Hesitation gone, I step into the front room.

"Release that dog!" I order.

Roy moves through me and reaches into the cloud. After a brief tug-of-war with the cloud, Roy stands up straight holding a quivering ball of black fur. Once free, the dog barks several times and struggles to reach Paige.

"Oh, hush," says Paige, "or I'll have you cast out back again and leave you there this time."

The dog stops barking and growls at her.

I silently cheer him on.

Several demons that were part of the cloud wind themselves around Roy's legs. One tries to enter him but bounces off harmlessly.

"Don't bother with him," says Paige. "He's sealed."

Her words ease me until she continues.

"Escort him into the room with our other guest. He can wait with her while Allister and I discuss his fate."

"You can't harm him." The reminder's as much for me as her. I try to draw comfort from it but get nothing.

More demons wrap around Roy, encircling his waist like a rope and dragging him into a room off to the left. He looks frightened, but at least there's still a defiant glint in his eyes.

Paige makes a dismissive noise.

"I can't harm his spirit, but I can still kill him," she says casually. To prove her point, Paige takes her human form and looks down at her purple-painted fingernails. "You'd be surprised how dangerous these things can be." She waves and turns her right hand, so I get a clearer view of the sharp tips.

My sigh contains a lot of frustration.

"Can we skip to the part where you tell me what you want, and I tell you I can't give it to you?" I ask.

"Don't underestimate yourself," says Paige. "You have no idea what I want. If you desire answers, please put that silly sword away and follow Roy. It's rude to keep the other guest waiting."

Though I know Paige has access to the universal knowledge same as I do, I find it troubling that she knows Roy's name.

Tyre's not really doing me much good, but I'm reluctant to send him away. However, the promise of answers is alluring. Tucking Tyre back into the Veil, I return to human form. This time, I add a light leather jacket to my usual jeans and T-shirt. My arms might need the added protection if I end up fighting Paige the old-fashioned way. Those nails look like weapons.

The air is thick with demons, but they clear a path for me. A memory of something similar happening ambushes me, but I'm aware it doesn't belong to me.

Mina's troubles began like this today.

Emboldened, I step into the living room. Roy sits on a couch next to a rocking chair, still clutching the black lab puppy. The dog probably can't see the demons, but he can certainly sense them. The hairs along his neck stand straight out and he rumbles like an idling engine.

The wooden rocking chair holds a chained woman. Her features match those Paige wore while answering the door for us. The sight of the chains doesn't necessarily shock me, but the amount of them does. Her arms and legs both have many layers of thick chains connecting them to various parts of the chair. More shiny links wrap her torso and chest. There's even a loop around her neck.

"Don't you think that's excessive?" I ask, working hard for a neutral tone.

"Don't let looks deceive you," says Paige. "I believe introductions are in order. Allister Knight, this is Lady Elizabeth Codee. She never goes by her first name anymore. She hasn't in ages. You have more in common than you know."

If Paige says anything else, I don't hear it. My attention stays with the bound woman. Something about her feels familiar. Her skin may appear wrinkled with age, but the sadness in her eyes goes deeper.

"Are you listening to me, Allister?" Paige demands. Her voice sails high with indignation.

Shaking myself, I refocus on Paige.

"I thought this history would interest you since it's likely to be your future."

Normally, a riddle like that would anger me, but my mind races along with my heart.

"You used to have a Kindred Spirit Bond." I speak the revelation softly, knowing there's potential to cause pain with them.

Lady Codee's eyes glisten with tears, but she nods slowly.

"She did," Paige confirms. "Until about fifteen years ago when she released it to deprive my master of its power." Paige pauses to study the woman. "This is what's left, a broken angel with diminished powers." She looks to me and adds, "Now you know the dangers of love."

"What are you yammering about?" I ask.

"What do you think brought her to this?" Paige counters, waving to the many chains holding Lady Codee. "Love. That's what." At my blank stare, Paige clutches her head like she has a massive headache. She grunts. "You are so thick!"

My brain keeps clicking away at the mental puzzle pieces.

"Who was your other half?" I ask Lady Codee, ignoring Paige's rant.

Strangely, the question mollifies Paige, bringing her frustration down to a simmer.

"Finally, an intelligent question," she mutters. She waves, and the chain around Lady Codee's neck loosens.

Something in my spirit speaks the name in concert with the prisoner's quiet answer.

"Josiah."

Fifteen years! The figure blazes in my mind. The implication that Master Josiah has been gone such a long time is staggering. The task of finding him seems more impossible than ever.

"Wonderful!" Paige cheers. "Now that that's out of the way, we can get down to business."

"What business?" I really don't want to ask that question.

"The business where I tell you what I want and you give it to me," Paige says darkly. "Unless you want this to be your fate too."

She's not referring to the chains. She's talking about the brokenness and sense of loss in Lady Codee.

"What do you want?" Roy voices the question, which is fine because it gets stuck in my throat.

Paige directs her answer to me.

"I want you to call Reena and convince her to tell us where Mina is headed. Once I have her, these two can go free."

Chapter 16:
Do Not Repeat Mistakes

Dear Lord Hadeon,

Thank you for the opportunity to serve the Dark Master openly. You will not regret it. The angelings' friend is with Deimos. I think he intends to keep her in the same spirit cell the girl occupied.

Concerning the angelings themselves, I am pleased to report partial success.

I had my doubts about Daeva's plan to capture Allister, but it's gone well so far. She is with the boy now in the same safehouse the girl fled from. Demons from Daeva's legion are with her to provide support and mine surround the house to prevent an escape.

Speaking of escape, why did your orders say to let the girl go? We could have had them both by now. I'm not questioning your wisdom, but the demons with me were not able to touch her, so there are no soul fragments to aid with locating her. We made brief contact, but I could not concentrate enough to detach a piece of my soul as a marker. I'm sorry to say that tracking the girl will take us some time. I wish I'd thought to have Lady Codee put a human tracking device on the girl.

Daeva assures me the boy will help us, but I think she may be underestimating his devotion to the girl. I don't know much of the history involving the last Kindred Spirit Pair, but the boy seems likely to choose a path like the one Lady Codee did. If I'm not mistaken, she severed the connection with her partner rather than risk his life or soul. Is that your intent? Whatever happened to the lady's other half?

What shall I do with the human who came with the boy? He has The Sight and has witnessed much tonight. As Daeva pointed out to the boy, I can kill the man if I do so in human form, but he has a holy seal. Would that not be a kindness to him?

The dog is showing usual resistance to becoming a host, but I'm not worried yet. Daeva wanted to kill the dog, but he may be useful as a hostage later. Humans grow very tight bonds to their pets, and I believe this might be true for the girl. She has spent several weeks in human form.

I will report again when we are fully successful. Meanwhile, I'm sure I speak for both of us when I say we would welcome any further insights and instructions you have.

Your devoted spymaster,
Than

***

Dear Than,

Do not let your eagerness to impress me outpace your results.

Finding Allister is indeed worth celebrating, but he is not yet a captive. Daeva's skills are adequate, but her mission will not be simple. An angel the boy has just met, a human, and a dog are not very strong leverage pieces. Daeva must convince the boy that her plan is in the girl's best interest or he will break free.

Deimos confirmed your delivery of Aderes and complimented you on your professionalism. He does not waste praise, so savor the thought.

I will answer most of your inane questions so you

97

can concentrate on your current tasks instead of wasting time with these side musings. Be grateful my patience has had time to grow, or we would be having a very different correspondence right now.

Short answers first. Do what you wish with the human and the dog once they have served their purpose. Kill them or free them. This job has few enough simple pleasures. Enjoy the power over life and death.

I told you to let the girl go because running will exhaust her mentally and physically. That will allow Spirit's Bane to quicken its work within her, and hopefully, make my job easier later.

I should not have to reiterate these facts. At full strength, the Kindred Spirit Pair is quite formidable. These angelings do not yet know the depths of power they can tap into together, and I'd like to keep it that way.

To that end, remind Daeva not to let Allister speak openly with Lady Elizabeth Codee. In fact, have the lady delivered to Deimos as soon as possible. He may be able to use her to exert some control over Adira Clarimond. They were very close friends before the incident that broke the last Kindred Spirit Bond. The Council of Light is currently embroiled in conflict that renders them practically useless, but I expect Clarimond to bring them to heel soon enough. Never waste potential resources.

Josiah is safe. His spirit has been moved to a secure location, which I shall not reveal. Do not inquire about it. His physical form is imprisoned on Earth. The split was an unforeseen consequence of the bond's violent end. I did some of my finest work during those months, but the event was both a crowning achievement and a devastating setback. At the time, we mistakenly believed destroying a Kindred Spirit Bond would end the matter, not simply release it to form in a new pair.

Before you ask, Codee did not tell her full tale to the Council of Light because she does not remember it. The Dark Master helped me suppress the remains of her memories. The effects are wearing off, so bits and pieces return to her. That is of no consequence. We always knew that would happen eventually. It was a fantastic opportunity while it lasted. The agent we sent to impersonate Josiah provided invaluable intelligence for quite a few years.

You must understand that although it's possible to quietly dissolve a Kindred Spirit Bond, that is not what happened between Codee and Josiah. I first captured one precious to them and then baited a trap, much as you and Daeva are planning for Allister and Mina. The hope, of course, was that they would join us, but when the time came, Codee directed considerable power inward, intent on resetting herself to save Josiah. He interfered. The power had nowhere to go. As a result, the bond shattered, Codee lost access to most of her Gifts, and Josiah's body and spirit split into two entities.

That should not have been possible, but I cannot change facts.

While we fought Josiah's spirit, Codee escaped with his human form and hid him on Earth. We only captured her again when she returned for his spirit. She would not betray the hiding place for anything, and I suspect she genuinely could not. The broken bond's effects were still manifesting. That's when we suppressed the rest of her memories of the incident and returned her to Adira and the Council of Light in the care of our agent. I don't know what he told them as I had not yet achieved my current position. Besides, he reported directly to the Dark Master, not my predecessor.

A word of caution you should draw from this bit of history: do not repeat these mistakes. I want this new Kindred Spirit Bond dissolved very gently. I'd like to repurpose it, and I cannot do that if it shatters again.

Things must happen in a certain order. The boy and girl must surrender and be taken to separate locations. One or the other must agree to dissolve the bond between them. The connection between them must be severed. Only after these things have transpired do I want to see the girl so I may conclude this business with Spirit's Bane.

The Dark Master has his eye upon us. I need not remind you that there are consequences for failure.

Hadeon, Servant of the Dark Master,
Director of Operations

Part 3:
Pressure

Chapter 17:
Violent Solution

Case Report #: MN-122
Case Agents: Master Blaz and Mistress Codee
Guardian: Mina Nadir

After boarding the train for Pittsburgh, I find a window seat and place my backpack under my legs so it won't be in the way if somebody wishes to sit next to me. I could put it in the overhead storage, but I prefer keeping it close to me. I should rest, but having never been on a train before, the sights and sounds fascinate me.

The low murmur of voices mingles with the shuffle of moving people and the hisses and sighs of the train itself. Rushing air is a constant background companion as blowers and fans try to maintain a comfortable temperature.

At first, there's a rush for seats. People can choose their own seats unless they bought a first-class ticket since those are assigned. The way passengers distribute themselves is interesting. Generally, groups sit together, but both groups and individuals try to avoid other people.

A young man wearing a suit takes the window seat directly opposite the one I chose. A mother with two boys takes the seat in front of him. Seeing this, the young man gets up and retreats three rows. I consider doing the same as one boy bashes the other with a plastic toy. Retaliation comes in the form of a fist to the first child's chin. Both children scream and cry while the woman wedges herself between them, alternating between scolding and comforting.

Reaching out with my spirit, I strengthen the woman's patience and soothe the boys. I'm careful not to alter the situation too much, but at least the piercing screams have subsided. It continually intrigues me that Spirit's Bane won't allow a shift to spirit form but merely aches slightly when I use certain gifts.

A teenage girl takes the seat the young man fled, oblivious to the recent turmoil. I wonder why until I see the little black earpiece. Her head bobs regularly in time to whatever she's listening to. The outside noise won't be bothering her for a while.

Curious, I stand and peer up and down the aisle. I want to know how many people are staring down at a phone. I can't see everybody, but it wouldn't surprise me to discover that the mother of the two boys and I are the only ones not engaged with a phone. She's still busy keeping the peace, and I don't have a phone. Lady C. and I discussed getting one for me, but I wanted to concentrate on my work instead of being lulled by pretty distractions.

A sense of sadness creeps over me. I don't need to mentally eavesdrop on my fellow passengers to tell that they're missing out on a lot of interaction time. Don't they realize how quickly life will pass?

The ability to think forward kicks in as I contemplate the spirits around me. Several fates play out for each one in the form of rapidly changing images. The overall effect disorients me, so I narrow the focus to the young man who moved seats to escape the small family.

Paul Kepler is on his way to audition for a violin spot in the Pittsburgh Symphony Orchestra. He's desperately trying not to think about what happens if he fails to get the single open position. He's also worried the papercut on his left ring finger won't heal properly in time. Thinking forward lets me see three possibilities: Paul obtaining his dream job, becoming an alternate, and being outright rejected. From the brief glimpses, becoming an alternate will be the best for him overall. I have no control over which future will happen in a situation like this, but I can help with the papercut. He's already dozing, so the healing

103

goes smoothly.

As the train begins moving, three unattached demons come into the car. Trying not to react to their presence, I monitor their progress through the passengers. They entered from the back and work their way forward, looking for opportunities to cause trouble. I can't tell their specialties until they're closer. They stop near Paul. Even in his semi-conscious state, his stress level spikes, telling me at least one is an Anxiety demon.

"You should give up. They don't want you," says one demon. His voice is gentle and comforting.

"You'll never be good enough," whispers another demon. He sounds more practical.

"You poor thing, all that worry is just piling up." The third demon's voice is female. "Shall we see if we can get a drink somewhere? Maybe a quick trip to the restroom for a vaping fix? That always helps your nerves."

I'm kind of shocked that the Despair demon employs such a kind voice. The Anxiety and Addiction demons sound closer to how I imagined they would. After weighing the consequences, I lend Paul some spiritual fortitude to withstand the harsh words he's enduring. The individual words might not stick with him, but the weight of them will still fall on his conscience anyway.

The demons spend several minutes working on him before concluding there might be easier targets.

When they reach me, I pretend to be asleep, but the first probing attack from the Despair demon gets quickly rebuffed. Since I'm not fully human, I don't have a holy seal that would warn the demon he cannot enter me. The resulting contact is brief but painful, outing me as an angel.

One of the demons freezes time. They're not as efficient at it as Allister or I would be, but the clumsy effort succeeds eventually. I refrain from helping or hindering them because I do not want them to know my abilities. I take in the three demons and try to think of the best way to get rid of them. If I turn to spirit, I could microjump them off the train then hop back on. That would work unless one of them has a Gift for teleportation too.

"Greetings, Guardian," says the Despair demon. "We

haven't seen your kind on this route in years. To what do we owe the pleasure of this visit?"

"I needed to be elsewhere," I answer.

"But why travel as a human?" wonders the Addiction demon. "Unless—"

"It's her." The Anxiety demon's excited conclusion dawns on the three simultaneously.

They immediately draw spirit weapons and level them at me.

"Please. I don't want trouble, but I will defend myself," I say. Standing as best I can in the small space, I face the demons.

The Addiction demon transforms into smoke and floats rapidly toward the back of the train car. The other two continue to guard me. I don't know their intent, but I gather the Addiction demon is summoning help.

I think forward the situation. A peaceful solution seems unlikely. The delight I sense in these demons tells me they've been promised great rewards for finding me. As when I faced Abdon, part of me wants to go with them, but I'm not ready yet. A violent solution will have consequences, but it is my only viable option. Letting the Addiction demon call in reinforcements will only make matters worse.

Calling Kentaro to me, I turn both hands to spirit to catch my sword and swing him like a bat at the Despair demon to my left. He shrieks as the katana crashes into his sword and forces both to pierce him. The combined impact resets him. He disappears before his smoky form hits the floor.

The Anxiety demon cries out defiantly and slashes downward with his two daggers. I yank Kentaro back into place in time and swing up to halt both weapons. Then, reaching into the part of time still steadily moving on, I reverse it two seconds. The humans won't know the difference since one of the demons already froze time on their plane. The only change is the position of the Addiction demon. She reforms directly behind the Anxiety demon.

I send Kentaro away and call him back immediately. The result is a split-second where the Anxiety demon stands like a statue before me, off balance because there's nothing resisting him anymore. When Kentaro reappears, he automatically moves through both demons to rest once again in my hands.

Shock registers in the Anxiety demon's expression before reset takes him. The Addiction demon slides backwards off the spirit sword with a hiss. Three shards—pieces of hardened shadow—sail through the dissipating remains of the Anxiety demon.

I flick two aside with Kentaro and duck the third. They would sting if they struck me, but they're not meant as a weapon against angels.

We stare at each other. Shadow wisps leak from the wound on her stomach. She conjures another shard and steps back until she's even with Paul.

"One wrong move and he dies," says the Addiction demon. "Maybe not today, but soon. This is a strong heroin craving."

I raise my hands in a non-threatening manner and pray silently for Tyre. As long as Allister's not currently using him, there's a chance the spirit sword will come to me.

"Vow to not speak of this and you may go," I say. "There's no need to hurt anybody."

"I disagree." Tossing me a hate-filled look, the Addiction demon slams the shard into Paul's neck.

He twitches but remains asleep.

"Save him or follow me. Your choice." The Addiction demon whirls and darts toward the back of the car.

A small tear forms in the Veil, letting Tyre through. I microjump to the far end of the car and bid the spirit sword to follow. With Tyre acting as a distraction, I swipe Kentaro clear through the Addiction demon.

Before her shriek fades, I'm back by Paul's side. Quickly, I place one hand on his chest and the other over his neck where the shard entered. His skin feels cold and clammy. Hoping I'm not too late, I sift through his spirit and use Spirit's Bane to pull the shadow fragments toward my hands. It's like using a strong magnet to draw out iron filings. The darkness in the shard is attracted to the power within the pendant. I provide a physical means for the shard fragments to reach Spirit's Bane. Then, carefully, I press Kentaro to the pendant until the shadow pieces disintegrate.

Exhausted, I thank Tyre and let him return to the Veil. Next, I release the hold on Kentaro, reform my human hands, return to my seat, and let time on the train proceed at a normal rate. Predictably, Spirit's Bane punishes me for the exertion since the time manipulation and most of my recent activities involved much of my spirit. I collapse onto the seat and close my eyes tight, trying to let the pain move through me.

It doesn't.

Instead, it moves to different parts of my body. Usually, it's sharp and stays in my chest, but this time, after a typical start, it changes to a dull ache and moves to my arms and legs. I'm glad much of the ride lies ahead of us because I don't think I could stand right now. My fingers swell up and become painful to bend. I'm forced to slip into spirit to heal them, which returns the pain to my chest. This time, it goes away like normal for several minutes before returning as a stabbing sensation in my stomach. Sweat dampens my palms and hair as I endure the new attack.

"Are you all right?" The question comes from a uniformed man.

I assure him the pain I'm experiencing is something I'm used to. He offers to fetch me some water. I let him because it gives me a moment to find my ticket. He hasn't asked for it yet, but I'm sure he will. I want to have the ticket ready because if he saw how much my hands tremble with each movement, he'd have more questions.

By the time the kind conductor returns with a bottle of water for me, I have somewhat mastered the pain. Convincing the man I won't die on his train takes some effort, but eventually, he continues with his rounds, promising to check in as soon as he can.

The length and severity of these episodes concerns me. Sleep is hard to achieve due to flareups, but I manage to rest for a few hours.

Chapter 18:
Possession

Case Report #: AK-122
Case Agent: Mistress Adira Clarimond
Guardian: Allister Knight

I laugh in Paige's face. Roy and the dog look at me curiously. Lady Elizabeth Codee's expression has not changed much. Several demons hover near Roy and the dog. The rest congregate near the ceiling, awaiting further orders.

"I'm not helping you find Mina," I say.

"You have no choice," Paige reasons. "I have almost a thousand demons inside this dwelling and another two thousand surrounding this place. There's no way for you to escape and preserve these lives."

"What makes me responsible for them?" I ask.

Roy casts a worried glance at me.

I avoid looking at him, but silently hope he trusts me.

The dog whines softly and tries to wriggle free and get to Lady Codee.

"I suppose nothing," Paige admits, "but that's surprisingly cold for you. Are you sure you're serving the right master?"

"I'm sure," I reply. "Maybe—"

I cut myself off, switch to spirit form, and microjump into Roy. Demons make that part look easy, but the first few seconds of possession, for lack of a kinder term, are confusing and awkward. Naturally, Roy's spirit fights me for control of his body, but I have a lot more experience at wrestling spirits. I'm going to owe him one very big apology later, but right now, I'm more concerned with the next step: getting very far away from Paige.

Before Paige can catch on, I have Roy tuck the dog close to his chest and revert to the last place I'd officially teleported to: Cold Spring, New York. Roy's body thuds to the ground next to the highway where we began the evening many hours before. Not comfortable with our proximity to the road, I microjump us past the line of nearby trees. Roy almost lands on his feet, but the added weight of the puppy throws him forward.

Disentangling our spirits, I move clear of Roy, take my human form, and reach out to steady him.

He staggers but soon catches his balance and slaps my hand away. The moonlight outlines enough of his stance to convey his anger. His breaths come in ragged gasps.

I want to apologize but decide to give him time to smolder first. Wordlessly, I pull the puppy free of Roy's grasp and examine him from every side. He appears whole. Releasing a worried breath, I lean him on my chest. The pup cranes his neck and starts licking my chin. I tuck him under my arm and turn back to Roy. I've transported other spirits before, but not many objects and certainly not mortal beings.

"What was that about?" Roy demands.

"I'm sorry," I say.

"Did you even think that plan through?" he continues.

"Not much," I admit, wincing at the unhelpful nature of the statement. "Paige wasn't much for hospitality, and I didn't want to leave you alone with her."

"We coulda died!" Roy's shout tells me he probably isn't hearing my explanations. "We could still die! Where are we anyway?" He turns a few circles and stares intently at the trees around us.

"Cold Spring," I answer. "Don't you recognize the road?"

Roy glares.

"Oh, I'm sorry. I musta missed the welcome sign when my body was being hijacked by an angel and dumped miles from my last location."

"We'll figure this out, Roy," I promise.

The dog adds a bark, though I'm not sure which side he's supporting.

A new thought strikes Roy, causing him to stand stiffer.

"You left that old lady with the crazy demon," he accuses.

I grimace at the reminder.

"I didn't want to leave her, but the spirit chains she wore would have made transporting her impossible," I explain.

"It still ain't right," Roy mutters.

"Not much about this is," I agree.

Silence falls between us.

I try to think forward the problem but keep getting blocked by worry for Mina. Paige could have been lying about the forces under her command, but I believe her. Three thousand demons is a sizable amount to be undertaking one hunt. We'll need to avoid them and get to Mina first, but what then? We're good, but I don't like to think of our odds of winning against a force that large.

Taking advantage of my distraction, the dog jumps down from my arms and darts off into the bushes to my right.

"Hey!" calls Roy.

"He's just taking care of some business," I say, watching the dog circle a tree.

After three circuits, he pauses, lifts a back leg, and waters the tree.

"Thanks fer saving me," says Roy.

The words sound like they pain him, but I have the sense not to point that out.

"What are we gonna do now?" Roy wonders. "We left my bike behind."

"Sorry about that," I say.

Roy waves off the apology.

"She'll be safe enough in that driveway, I guess," he says. "It's us I'm worried about. How are we gonna find your friend? And how are we gonna get to her?"

"You're not going to like my answer to the second question," I tell Roy. Frowning, I add, "And I don't like the answer to the first question."

"Why not?" asks Roy.

"Because Paige came up with it," I say.

Reena may not know where to find Mina, but she could probably convince Lady A. to share the information with her. Not wanting to delay any longer, I reach out to Reena. My telepathy abilities aren't good enough to hold a conversation with her, but she's kind enough to answer the call by teleporting to us.

"How will—"

Reena's sudden appearance cuts off Roy's question.

He clutches his chest and sucks in a sharp breath.

Upon finding I have company, Reena's two short swords spring out of the Veil and into her hands.

"He's with me," I say, microjumping in front of Roy.

"How do I know you're you?" asks Reena.

With the high number of shapeshifting and illusion-wielding demons we've run into lately, it's a fair question and a solid reminder. The low, even pitch to Reena's voice certainly sounds as it should, but she too could be an imposter.

"You don't, but I need to find Mina," I say quickly. "Her first safehouse was compromised. Help me find where she would go. How do you want me to prove myself?"

Changing to spirit, Reena moves through me. The contact is strange but not painful, as it would be if either one of us were demons.

"I am satisfied," Reena concludes, "but unfortunately, I can't help you. For her safety, I never knew the other locations. Only Mistress Clarimond could give you what you seek."

"How is she?" I blurt the question before Reena can teleport back to the Heavens.

"Holding her own," Reena reports in a cautious tone.

"Can you ask her to help me?" I inquire. "I'm going to find Mina some other way, but if Paige was right, there are a lot of demons after us."

Reena stares at me for a few seconds as she weighs my request.

"Would you like me to mark you?" she asks at last.

"Please," I answer. "A mark will let her teleport directly to my location," I explain for Roy's benefit.

Reena wastes no time placing a hand on my right shoulder. Bowing her head, she mouths some words silently.

Warmth spreads from the spot she touched, but it vanishes a second later when she teleports away.

"This day's getting stranger by the second," Roy comments. "What do you wanna do with the dog?"

"We need to take him somewhere safe," I answer.

Another brief silence forms. It's broken by Roy clearing his throat.

"We could take him to my ma," says Roy. "We had to put down our buddy Booster a few months ago, but I think she's still got all the stuff to care for a dog."

Kneeling, Roy calls the puppy over.

"Come here, feller," says Roy. "We don't even know what to call ya."

When the dog trots over, Roy checks the tag attached to his collar and scoops him up.

"Takoda. Can't say I've ever met a Takoda before, but it suits ya," says Roy.

The name makes me smile. Its meaning of "friend to everyone" sounds like something Mina would choose.

"Come on. Do your creepy possession thing," Roy prompts. "We should get this feller to safety then find yer lady friend."

His phrasing stops me.

"I'm taking you both home," I tell Roy. "This isn't your fight."

"That pretty demon made it my fight when she threatened that old lady," Roy says fiercely.

I refrain from telling Roy that the "old lady" is an angel who doesn't need his protection. Besides, maybe she does. There's a chance Paige leaves Lady Codee behind while pursuing Mina, but it's slim at best. If it boils down to a confrontation of any sort, Mina will have my attention, and I can't be everywhere at once. Roy's already proven to have a strong spirit, and I'm guessing he's a decent prayer warrior.

"Are you sure you want to come?" I ask, giving him the chance to back away. "You've already done more than your duty as my guide."

Takoda barks impatiently.

"You're not coming," I tell the dog, still waiting for an

answer from Roy.

"Maybe he should," Roy comments. "The demons at the house couldn't control him. He might be able to distract some of them."

I consider the logic and study the plea in the puppy's eyes. My resolve wavers then solidifies as I picture Mina's worried face. I am not going to be the guy who got her puppy killed.

"I think we have enough to keep track of," I tell Roy. "Let's tuck this little guy away so Mina has a loved one to return to."

Chapter 19:
Sister

Case Report #: MN-123
Case Agents: Master Blaz and Mistress Codee
Guardian: Mina Nadir

By the time the train finally pulls into the Grant Street Transportation Center in Pittsburgh, my Spirit's Bane problems have worsened to the point I'm not sure I'll be able to disembark without help. My legs ache a lot. I absently rub them while the other passengers gather their belongings and exit.

"What's wrong with her, Momma?" asks one of the young boys.

"She's all sweaty," pipes up his brother.

"Is she gonna throw up?" asks the first boy.

Maybe. I silently answer. My stomach flips at the possibility. *I sure hope not.*

The woman shushes her sons and hustles them past me like lingering would allow them to catch something deadly. Her concerned, almost embarrassed, expression makes me wonder what I look like.

I chuckle at the short exchange, even though it hurts. Children are refreshingly honest. With effort, I turn my head left to check my appearance in the window glass. It's not a vanity thing. I obviously need to make some adjustments, so I don't draw too much attention to myself.

The kind conductor returns to check on me. His primary emotions are a strange mixture of concern and relief, but he forces a smile for my benefit.

"You'll be all right now, miss," he says. "I was going to call an ambulance for you, but your sister said she'd take care of that."

Sister?

The question barely forms in my head before the man shifts enough to let me spot Paige standing behind him. She's wearing jeans and a blue University of Pittsburgh sweatshirt. Her blond hair has been swept back into a loose ponytail. We don't look much like sisters, but then again, I don't know what the conductor sees when he looks at her. If she possesses the right Gifts, he could very well be seeing a mirror image of me.

"It's so good to see you!" Paige says brightly.

The greeting is mostly for the conductor's ears, but the words have a ring of truth to them.

I'm instantly wary.

"You don't know how long I've looked for you." Her statement contains enough concern and annoyance to sound genuine. She squeezes past the conductor, plops down on the seat next to me, and pulls me into a hug.

A chill shoots through Spirit's Bane and spreads quickly throughout my body. I can tell Paige did something to me, but I can't imagine what.

"Play the part," she adds in a whisper. Her tone implies a threat though she doesn't elaborate.

"Do you need help with her?" the conductor asks Paige. "I can carry her off the train and call for a wheelchair if you like."

Releasing me, Paige turns to the conductor.

"That would be lovely," she says, "but I don't think we need a wheelchair. If you can help me get her off the train to a bench, we can manage from there. I'm sure she's just exhausted from the long ride."

"I don't know, ma'am," says the conductor. "She looks like a hospital visit would do her good."

"I'll be fine," I assure the conductor. Wanting to prove it, I struggle to a standing position. Because my backpack is still at my feet, the move causes me to crowd Paige.

Taking the hint, she slides back off the seat into the aisle, moving far enough back to give the conductor room to move in and reach for my arms.

"I'll grab her bag," says Paige.

The conductor nods and guides me into the aisle. Once there, he moves my left arm close to my body and loops his right arm around my back, providing support.

My legs feel shaky, but they hold. The narrow passageway feels cramped, but the conductor skillfully leads me off, still half-supporting my weight.

"May I pick you up to carry you down the stairs?" asks the conductor.

"Of course!" Paige answers for me.

He waits for my permission, so I give it.

"Hold on to my neck, please," he instructs, leaning down to pick up my legs.

I'm worried the exertion will give the man a heart attack. He's breathing almost as hard as I am, but in a few short seconds, the conductor sets me on my feet and helps me hobble over to a nearby bench.

Once more, he offers to fetch a wheelchair, but we politely decline. He'll be much safer far away from us. After a few rounds of thanks and assurances, the conductor tips his hat to us and climbs back on the train.

As soon as we're alone, Paige grabs my hand and teleports us to an empty conference room. I think we're in the same building, but I can't be certain. Besides, the location doesn't change much about my situation.

Paige deposits me in a high-backed leather chair.

I stare at her and try to gauge my chances of teleporting someplace she can't follow.

"Don't bother teleporting anywhere," Paige advises. "It's only going to anger me." She pokes Spirit's Bane, which lies beneath my sweatshirt. "I placed a small part of me in that. As long as you're wearing it, you'll never lose me."

"How did you find me?" I'm not completely convinced Paige is telling the truth, but I don't have the energy to run away yet anyway.

"When was the last time you ate?" Paige asks, ignoring my question. "You look awful."

"Thanks," I mumble. "It's been a rough few days."

"Abdon told me about the fight," says Paige. "You know he let you escape, right?"

"I think I ate this morning," I say, instead of acknowledging her rhetorical question. "I slept as much as I could on the train. Guess eating slipped my mind."

"You have to take better care of yourself," Paige says. She pulls two pairs of metal handcuffs from the Veil and applies one to each of my wrists, securing them to the arms of the chair.

I give her a curious look for several reasons. First, the handcuffs are useless. They're not spirit cuffs, so escaping them would take less time than it takes to form the thought. Second, she seems to be waiting for something, and third, her emotions don't match her actions.

"Last I checked we play for different teams," I note. "Why are you concerned with my health?"

Paige makes a show of checking her phone for the time.

"Allister's probably going to take a few more hours to find us," says Paige. "We have some time to kill. Wait here and I'll grab us some burgers."

Before I can reply, Paige disappears.

I turn my hands to spirit to slip out of the handcuffs, but she's back before I work up to sitting up straight.

"That was freakishly fast," I say.

"I ordered ahead," Paige explains. She slides a burger over to me.

The food smells wonderful, but I don't feel like eating. I'd much rather find a hole somewhere and sleep for a few weeks.

"Eat," Paige orders. Opening the wrapper on a second burger, she takes a large bite. "It's good, and it'll probably make you feel better."

"I doubt it," I say as Spirit's Bane sends a short stabbing pain through me for the move that let me slip out of the handcuffs.

Paige consumes half her meal before renewing her you-should-eat campaign.

"Eat and I'll consider answering some of your questions," she offers.

It's a surprisingly fair deal, so I take it.

"Start with how you found me," I prompt, unwrapping the burger.

"You and Allister aren't exactly subtle," Paige comments, "and you have a unique fighting style."

As I fulfill my side of the eating bargain, Paige explains that she first tried to get Allister to tell her where to find the new safehouse. When that failed because he doesn't know where to find it, she turned to the incident reports and human surveillance networks.

"Demons being reset would mean little," says Paige. "Same thing for glitches with surveillance cameras on trains, but the combination was worth investigating." She finishes her meal, crumples up the wrapper, and tosses it over to the trash bin in the far corner. Her aim was off, but the wrapper alters course and ends up where she wanted it to go anyway. "It wasn't the only event I had checked, but I got lucky. A Sloth demon inhabiting one of the passengers witnessed the altercation. He said you were brilliant and described the fight in detail."

I shake my head and take my frustration out on the empty burger wrapper. How could I have missed something so simple? I didn't even think to check for other demons already inhabiting a human host. I wouldn't have done anything preemptively, but I might have been able to silence them if I'd considered them a threat.

"Don't be too hard on yourself," says Paige. She pulls my empty wrapper across the table and sends it on the same path as hers took.

Propping my elbow on the table, I lean my forehead on the heel of my palm.

"Why are you being nice to me, and what do you want?" I ask, not bothering to look at Paige.

"I'd like to convince you to wear spirit cuffs," Paige says conversationally.

"Not happening, but go on," I say.

"And I'm being nice to you because it's a lot easier than chasing you."

"You're waiting for something," I point out. Lifting my head, I meet her gaze. "If it's Allister, I won't help you."

Paige chuckles.

"He said something similar, but as I informed him, you have no choice." She bestows a compassionate look upon me. "As I said, now that you're marked, you can teleport to the far side of the world, and I'll still find you."

Her look hardens into something unpleasant. She glances at the handcuffs hanging from the chair. They snap open eagerly. Slowly, she gets up, saunters over, and pushes me gently back into the leather chair. Next, she reapplies the handcuffs.

"My orders are to deliver you and Allister to my master," Paige explains, returning to her seat. "Spirit's Bane is going to do most of my work for me. I honestly don't need you to do much besides stay in one place with me and use your Gifts. We could do this here, but I would much prefer the isolation of your new safehouse."

I shake my head once.

"I won't endanger others," I say, rejecting the idea of leading Paige to the safehouse. It's doubtful the location will harbor any other angels, except the caretaker, but the safehouse likely serves as a backup refuge for many.

"You will if you choose the hard way," Paige counters. "The only question is who the others will be, humans or angels."

Her words sink sharp teeth into my conscience. I want to ask her why she's doing this, but it's a dumb question.

"Here's how this will work," says Paige. Her tone flips back to pleasant. "We can stay in this conference room and play with handcuffs for a while, but I'll probably lose patience with the exercise. When that happens, I'll fetch a random human and hurt them. You'll get to play hero and save them. We'll rinse and repeat until Allister finds us. That's option one of the hard way."

She doesn't need to explain option two of the hard way, but she does anyway. It involves much the same methodology with angels as targets instead of humans.

My throat goes dry.

"What's the easy way?"

"You call to him," answers Paige. "Open your spirit to Allister, and he can teleport to us in an instant."

Chapter 20:
Stowaway

Case Report #: AK-123
Case Agent: Mistress Adira Clarimond
Guardian: Allister Knight

Not eager to inhabit Roy's body again, I try a few microjumps holding his right hand. He carries Takoda. Thankfully, it works. Since holding hands is very awkward, we try teleporting with me touching one of Roy's shoulders. When that works, I try again while hovering in his personal space. That does not work. A few jumps later, we conclude that I must touch some part of Roy for it to work. Even having both of us hold part of Takoda doesn't work. I simply end up microjumping with the dog and leaving Roy behind.

Satisfied, we jump for real. I remember where to find his mother's house, but I double-check the coordinates anyway. Though I aim for where I think the family room might be, we end up in the garage.

Leaping from Roy's arms, Takoda dashes around the small space, sniffing everything he can. The little black dog crashes into a toolbox and knocks over a broom. The handle catches the side of a hookboard, rattling its contents. Something falls off the board and lands near Takoda. The puppy growls and unleashes a long string of furious barks at the offending object, which turns out to be a spade.

"Roy! What—Where—Is that a dog?" his mother sputters. She stands in the doorway to the rest of the house, holding a frying pan across her chest.

Takoda stops barking and ducks behind my legs, peeking out to growl at the stranger. I want to reassure him, but I don't even know her name. As the fact occurs to me, her name pops into my head, much like road and town names appear when I teleport somewhere new.

I'm glad we're not real intruders. Ida May Santori might be short, but she looks ready to swing that frying pan with purpose.

"It's all right, Ma," Roy calls. "It's me an' Allister. You remember him, right?"

"Of course, I remember him. I'm not senile yet." Lowering the frying pan, Ida hustles out of the house. Shoving the pan into Roy's hands she wraps me up in a huge hug. After a brief but intense visual inspection, she pats my shoulders and stoops to greet Takoda. "Well, bless my soul. You're new."

"It's a long story," says Roy.

"Hells bells, y'all know how to make an entrance." Ida takes in the fallen broom and the chaotic state of the upended toolbox. "Thought the house was comin' down." Ida stands and stretches her back. "Before ya get to explainin', come on in an' sit down. Are ya hungry? I was just startin' to make some fried chicken for this afternoon's prayer meetin'."

Roy glances at a small clock on his workbench and gives his mother a strange look.

"It's 3:43 a.m.," he says. "Why are ya even awake?"

"Couldn't sleep. Besides, that chicken doesn't bread or fry itself," says Ida. She adjusts the belt of her silky bathrobe. "Now, I don't know about you boys, but I find this place drafty. I'm headed in. Y'all are welcomed to come in outta the night."

We follow Roy's ma into the house and sit down at the kitchen table. She grabs some large glasses and serves us sweet tea. Takoda explores the small kitchen before sitting down in front of the counter where about three pounds of chicken breasts are spread out in various states of being breaded.

Taking turns, Roy and I bring his mother up to speed on the night's activities. We cover Roy's search, my sudden

121

appearance, the ride to the diner, the trip to Mina's former safehouse, and the discovery that we can teleport together. I notice he skims over some details and downplays the danger, but since there's no point making his mother anxious, I do the same. As we bring our tale to a close, I subtly indicate that Roy should make our pitch. Luckily, he picks up on the signal and clears his throat nervously.

"We're headed back out to search for Mina soon, and we need ya to watch over Takoda," says Roy.

"He's welcomed to stay, but I don't think headin' out now is a good idea," says Ida. "Y'all need to get some rest first or risk being useless to that poor girl."

She's right. I can refresh my human body by staying in spirit for a short time, but Roy doesn't have that luxury. Once again, I consider leaving Roy behind. I'm anxious to get to Mina first, but not if I lead Paige to her. I can't very well fight for my friend and keep an eye on Roy. He's likely to end up dead.

A crazy plan pops into my head and drives off the despairing thoughts. I'll have to discuss it with Roy. It will take a lot of coordination and careful timing on my part, but it might give us the advantage if we end up tangling with Paige's insane number of demons.

"Can we afford a delay?" Roy asks me.

"Sure," I reply.

The deep lines under his eyes tell me he needs this.

"I need to make some arrangements anyway," I add.

"You stay. Wait for mistress." The raspy orders come from a little Chaos demon.

"How did you get in?" I ask. Launching myself to my feet, I turn to spirit and call Tyre to me.

"What's going on?" Ida stares right through me, telling me she doesn't have The Sight. "Roy? Where's Allister?"

Tapping into one of Mina's skills, I turn most of my body back into human form but keep my hands spirit so I can hold my sword.

The Chaos demon pokes at the container of breadcrumbs, causing it to tip over. He shakes his hands in victory before scampering over to the stove and playing with the dials.

"Get out of this house!" My command sounds sharper as I

channel my frustration.

The only way the demon could get in was on or in one of us. I should have checked for stowaways before we jumped. He probably didn't hitch a ride on me since I've taken spirit form before teleporting several times today. A mental image of demons wrapping around Roy's legs comes to me, and I wonder how the Chaos demon managed to go undetected.

"There's a small demon on the counter," Roy explains for his mother.

Ida's expression wavers between shock and irritation.

"Well, don't just stand there piddlin' around. Cast it out," she orders.

"He's trying," Roy assures her.

"Out. Now," I say to the demon.

When he picks up a book of matches, I microjump across the room and smack him with Tyre.

The Chaos demon leaps into the upper right corner of the room and hisses at me.

"We are legion. You are not," says the demon. "Surrender and they may live."

With a malicious smile, the Chaos demon splits into two.

Roy and I exchange a horrified look.

"Start praying," I say to Roy and his mother before completely taking my spirit form.

With a tight nod, Roy rushes to his mother's side and clasps hands with her.

By the time my attention returns to the Chaos demon, he's formed six smaller versions of himself. They're the size of large rodents.

"Last warning you're going to get," I say, waving toward the door.

The six mini demons swarm around me. I grip Tyre with both hands and close my eyes. A demon fragment slams into my right shoulder, causing a burning sensation. Two more aim for my back. I magnify my presence, causing a burst of light that stuns the Chaos demon. He freezes in fear. Tyre and I carve a swift, complicated path through the air, sweeping aside the demon fragments.

"More coming!" cries the demon defiantly as Tyre passes

through the last piece.

I let Tyre return home and become human once more.

Roy and Ida are shaken but fine. A short discussion results in a simple plan of action. Roy will sleep for a few hours. Ida will activate her prayer chain and see who can move the planned meeting up to this morning. I will see if Lady A. can speak with me. There's a lot to plan regardless of what Roy says when I officially ask for his help.

Roy heads to the den to take a nap, but I pull him aside.

"You don't have to come," I say. "Your ma might need you here."

"I'm seein' this through," Roy declares.

He doesn't look ready for a longer discussion, so I get out of his way. As he lays down, it occurs to me that the Chaos demon might not have been the only stowaway. Taking spirit form, I move through Roy. This is different than jumping into him. If I'd moved through him the first time, any demons on him would have fled from the contact between our spirits.

"Just checking for more demons," I say in answer to Roy's questioning look. "Sleep well."

In hindsight, that may not have been the most comforting way to end the conversation.

Before settling myself, I circle the house several times and erect several prayer barriers. Determined demons will still get in, but then, they'll have to contend with Ida Santori. I spend a few moments blessing Roy and his mother and strengthening their spirits.

Planning to deal with surprises Paige may pull takes me a few hours. I fail to contact Lady A., but Reena hears me out and agrees to help.

Roy's still asleep. So are Ida and Takoda.

Having done everything in my power to protect this dwelling, I too let my body rest.

Chapter 21:
Hard Way Three

Case Report #: MN-124
Case Agents: Master Blaz and Mistress Codee
Guardian: Mina Nadir

"How do you expect to contain Allister?" I ask Paige. It's not idle small talk. I need her to open up about herself so I can do something desperate and probably stupid. "No offense, but I'm not exactly in peak condition, and you're already resorting to threats."

"That's easy enough," says Paige. Her tone dips into sickeningly sweet territory. "I'll hurt you. You're immortal, not immune to pain."

Spirit's Bane takes the opportunity to remind me of that fact. I stare at Paige and concentrate on catching my breath. Sometimes, the pain lessens if I can alter my breathing pattern. This is not one of those times, so I merely endure.

"Do you ever get tired of threatening people?" I wonder, sitting back in the large leather chair.

Paige shrugs.

"Not really," she says. "I find it endlessly fascinating how different beings react to threats. It's really an art form to discover what kind of threat works best. For some, it's their significant other or their children. For others, it's the idea of embarrassment or scandal or the thought of pain." Genuine excitement comes through Paige's speech.

While she's distracted, I locate the mark she left on Spirit's Bane. Instead of destroying it, I trace it back to her and strengthen it into an invisible cord that connects us.

"How long have you enjoyed pain in others?" I wonder.

"Haven't you been listening to anything?" Paige scolds. "Pain is a tool, one of many. If I thought asking nicely would work, I'd go with it." She stops herself and shakes her head. "For the record, this is me asking nicely. I doubt it'll work, but when it fails, I'll at least be able to say I tried."

"Does that help your conscience?" I ask.

"Stop stalling, Mina," says Paige. "Make a decision. Easy way, hard way one, or hard way two?"

"None of the above," I answer.

Paige regards me carefully.

"I guess we could try hard way three," she muses.

"What's that?" I know the answer before Paige meets my eyes.

Reaching into the bag the burgers came in, Paige draws out a gun, aims for my left shoulder, and pulls the trigger.

I teleport.

It hurts, but I'm betting the pain is far less than having to heal a bullet wound.

I reappear in a large, empty field of grass, as planned. Looking startled, Paige appears the exact distance away from me as she was in the conference room in Pittsburgh, also as planned. She still has that gun. Not part of the plan, but to be expected.

As I wonder where exactly I've taken us, words appear in my mind: **Teague, Freestone County, Texas**.

Since I'd had less than a second to choose a destination, my only criteria had been far away from people with a lot of open space. Since the fields expand in every direction around us and the blue sky seems to go on forever, I at least got the open space part right.

Expression hardening, Paige fires again.

I spirit flash into her, reasserting human form as we meet. The result is a spectacular tackle that carries us at least fifty feet. We hit the ground and roll several times. Paige screeches like a bird of prey and punches me. I twitch my head left, but her fist still clips the side of my face on its way to meet the ground. Something snaps in her wrist and her rage-filled cry turns pained. Shoving her off, I scramble to my feet and move away from Paige.

She climbs to her feet and cradles her right wrist, which clearly shows a break. She must have put significant force behind that punch to do that kind of damage. My ears ring and my head aches, but a wave of pity sneaks up on me anyway. Ignoring it for a second, I once again strengthen the connection between Paige and me.

Fury in her eyes, Paige teleports away. A second later, she reappears.

I laugh with relief. The mirth dies when Paige spirit flashes into me. We sail through the air back toward our original landing site. Unfortunately, she lands on top. Her right arm is tucked close to her chest protectively, but that doesn't stop her from slapping me hard with her left hand.

With effort, I throw her off again and try to get to my feet. I manage to get to my knees before Spirit's Bane floods my pain sensors from head to toe. With a moan, I sink to the ground and curl into a ball. I land facing Paige, so I see her slowly recover her feet and stalk closer.

I try to move but can't.

She kicks me onto my back.

"What did you do?" Paige articulates each word carefully.

"I ... connected us," I admit.

Paige tries teleporting again. I don't know where she goes, but she's back two seconds later. Her surprise flips back to rage. Kneeling beside me, she grips my sweatshirt with her good hand.

"Undo it." She growls the order.

I shake my head, suddenly very weary.

"It's just you, me, and the fresh air," I say.

Paige lifts me up through my sweatshirt and slams me down again. The move jars my head, but since she only lifted me an inch or two, it doesn't hurt much.

"Why would you connect us?" asks Paige.

Her tone says she's merely voicing her frustrations, but I answer her anyway.

"So you can't hurt anybody." My eyes fall upon her twisted, broken wrist. "Except yourself." Instinctively, I reach out to touch the injured arm.

Paige catches my wrist with her good hand and looks at me fiercely. An understanding passes between us. She could snap my wrist in a heartbeat.

"Let me heal that for you," I say.

A gust of wind blows over us, casting dust into our faces. I close my eyes until it's over. When I open them again, I find Paige staring at the ground beside me lost in thought. She looks torn. There's a deep streak of pride within her that stands against accepting any form of help.

"Accepting aid is not a weakness," I say.

"Stop reading my mind," Paige snaps.

"I'm not," I assure her. "I'm reading your expression."

"Why would you help me?" she asks. "I got this fighting you."

"Because I can," I answer, struggling to find a satisfactory answer for myself. "And because it's right." That sounds ridiculous. "Or because maybe if I do, you'll realize we don't have to fight."

Keeping my movements slow, I pull my wrist free and place it delicately over the bruised section of Paige's arm. My chest burns as my Healing Gift asserts itself. She must have shattered several bones because the process takes almost a minute to complete. By the time I finish, there are tears in Paige's eyes. She blinks the tears away and flexes the hand. When our eyes meet again, there's a deep-seated sadness in her.

"Thank you," she whispers, "but this doesn't change my orders. I've chosen my side."

"Maybe you can change," I say.

Paige rejects the idea with a swift headshake and draws a pair of spirit cuffs out of the Veil. They look like ordinary silver handcuffs, but darkness emanates from them.

Dread settles heavily upon me. Having those cuffs on will force at least part of me to turn to spirit. Given my current condition, that will cause a tremendous amount of pain. Normally, such a weapon cannot be used without some degree of submission, but my weakened state may be enough of an opening.

"Don't make me use these on you." The plea in Paige's voice gives me hope for her. "Bring Allister here and get him to come with us."

"I ... can't do it." I shiver and try to brace myself.

Paige reaches for my arm, and I microjump a few feet away. Upon landing, I drop to a knee, dizzy from the effort.

"Stop running," Paige advises. "You're only hurting yourself."

I agree with her, but the need to continue fighting burns within me.

"Stop fighting," I counter. "You were made for more than hurting others."

Paige spirit flashes at me, but I dodge. She recovers the distance easily, but halts about ten feet away from me.

"I can keep doing this for days," says Paige, "but you can't."

Something warm and wet drips out of my nose as sharp pain explodes through my head, feeling like a sword went straight into my brain and scrambled it. I touch the wet spot and glance at my hand. My fingers come away bright red with blood. Concentrating as best I can, I stop the stream and wipe at the blood that's already fallen. The self-healing works, righting both my nose and my head, but causing a familiar response from Spirit's Bane. The pain drops me to my knees.

Paige spirit flashes to me and catches hold of my shoulders before I can fall over.

"You're so stubborn," she says, helping me to the ground. She looks exasperated. "I didn't think you'd really choose hard way three."

Chapter 22:
Trace and Trap

Case Report #: AK-124
Case Agent: Mistress Adira Clarimond
Guardian: Allister Knight

Roy's mother must be expecting a small army for the prayer meeting. Several large trays brimming with chicken line three counters and the bulk of the kitchen table. Despite the cool morning, the kitchen window stands wide open. Nevertheless, most of the house still smells like fried chicken.

Ida must have finally decided to rest before her guests arrive. A small sticky note near the sink tells me to help myself to chicken or anything in the refrigerator. It even describes where I can find the eggs and milk. I didn't think that would be necessary until I peek and discover that every millimeter of space is being used.

Deciding not to upset the delicate balance within the refrigerator, I select a large chicken breast from a tray on the table and eat it over the sink. While savoring the warm crunch of fried chicken, I ponder how to track Mina down. Normal methods are failing.

I'd hoped my connection with Mina would let me follow her despite whatever the Council did to dampen our connection when she went into hiding on Earth. That's not entirely fair. Although I want to blame the Council, the truth may be that my friend is actively masking her presence. Knowing Mina, she would see it as the only way to protect me from the problems plaguing her.

She's wrong. We need to face this together.

A sense of Mina appears and vanishes so quickly I barely have time to identify it, but once I do, I realize I've felt her several times in the last few hours. That convinces me she's actively burying our connection. Furthermore, whatever she did to hide her presence is weakening.

I need to find her soon. If I'm starting to detect her, other spirits will be able to do so shortly as well.

After the third time my thoughts run a futile circle, I turn to Reena. She's one of the few beings I trust enough to risk contacting right now. She is also kind enough to put aside the tasks I've given her to answer my summons. We have a brief but enlightening conversation.

Once I lay out my fears, Reena suggests I try locating Mina's Trace. When I express doubts, Reena corrects my understanding of Traces.

"Mina might be avoiding the Kindred Spirit connection, but perhaps she forgot to hide the rest of her presence. You don't need a strong connection to a person to recognize their essence," she explains. "How do you think you've been contacting me?"

"I figured it was through a minor Gift of telepathy," I say.

"That helps, but you're also identifying my presence and directing your thoughts to me," says Reena. "The same is true for how I found you in the woods near Cold Spring."

My expression must say I'm lost, but I voice the confusion anyway.

"If you could do that, why did you mark me?" I ask.

"Think of a mark as a very strong Trace," Reena says. "I use it because it's convenient, but as long as you're not altering anything, a Trace would work as well. There's a theory that as long as you've interacted with somebody, you mark their spirit and they mark yours."

"Is there a way to make the connection stronger?" I ask.

We debate the possibility for a minute, but then, I let Reena return to her duties. Roy should be awake soon.

We have to move quickly or Paige will find Mina first.

The thought stabs me painfully the first three times it

131

loops through my head.

On the fourth time, my breath hitches, and I see it in a new light.

Paige will find Mina first.

She has thousands of demons scouring the country for my friend. Given the disparity in our resources, the thought will soon be fact.

I've talked with Paige, and I've fought with her.

That means I can find her.

I drop to my knees right there in the kitchen. Closing my eyes, I let my thoughts dwell on Paige. I search my feelings to see if I can recognize her presence. Before the first time she picked a fight with me in the desert, we had very little to do with each other. If I needed an escort to my training activities, I tended to get Abdon. Paige accompanied Mina.

Nothing unique occurs to me until I use Mina's Empathy Gift. Once I do, a question burns in my mind and lights up my soul.

Is Paige a mole or a traitor?

Since the end result's the same, I don't understand why the distinction should matter. I'm exasperated to the point of frustration, but once I stop thinking the question stupid, I let myself dig into the difference.

A mole would be an enemy plant. If Paige is a mole, she's both highly skilled and probably trusted. If she's a traitor, she may be newer to the enemy's camp. In other words, she might be redeemable.

Could she not be both?

The thought sounds like Mina. In that moment, I get another very brief sense of her, but unlike the others, this feels more like a message: ***pray for her***.

Somehow, I understand that the *her* is Paige.

Why would Mina want me to pray for Paige?

We're enemies.

Though personally, I still have raging doubts, I follow the instinct to honor my friend.

My King. I don't know what to say. You know what choices Paige has made in her life. You know why and how she serves the Prince of Darkness. You also know what lies he told

132

her and if she's made an unchangeable decision or a fixable mistake. Show her mercy. If possible, draw her back into the light.

The guests arrive and the prayer meeting takes place. I spend it in spirit so as not to startle the humans. It does my heart good to hear their heartfelt pleas on our behalf, even though most of them do not know the situation.

The meeting stretches late into the afternoon.

When the prayer part ends, they spend some time sharing the food.

As the last guest leaves, I feel lighter and calmer, but more importantly, I can sense Paige. The feeling shines like a torch set on a hill on a moonless night.

I feel Mina again too. An odd sensation of relief and terror strikes me when I realize Mina and Paige's presence are coming from the same location.

Racing into the living room, I quickly rouse Roy who somehow slept right through the entire prayer meeting.

"Get up," I order. "I found them."

Despite my impatience, I give the man enough time to completely awaken before forcing him to throw water on his face and eat something. I use the time to explain my plan. He agrees to it and waits patiently while I make the final arrangements with Reena. Next, we wake his mother—who needed a nap after the prayer meeting—to let her know we're leaving. Truth is, what we plan to do carries insane risk. Ida deserves the chance to properly send her son into the fray.

I move a respectful distance away while they exchange some words.

When Roy's ready, he comes over and holds out his hand as if to shake. I double check my plan with him and gain his full cooperation.

Reena appears to do her part.

Finally, I clasp Roy's hand and teleport us to Texas.

We arrive in a field. The view of scrappy grass and short trees expands around us in every direction, but my attention immediately fixes on a disturbing scene.

Paige kneels over a body.

Sunlight glints off of something in her hands. My mind

jumps to a dagger, but the image doesn't fit. The silvery object feels darker. An ordinary dagger wouldn't feel like anything and a spirit dagger would only carry a faint reflection of its maker.

"Step away from that angel!" Roy orders.

Paige's head snaps up to take us in. I can't identify the emotion in her eyes, but it's quickly replaced by disdain.

"I'm surprised you brought a human into danger," Paige says, ignoring Roy. "And one with The Sight too." She eyes him with studied disinterest.

"I volunteered," Roy declares.

"Then, you're both brave and stupid," Paige concludes, "but thank you for coming. You can help me make Allister mind his manners."

Roy and I didn't exactly discuss what he would say, but I'm grateful Paige hasn't outright killed him.

Their exchange gives me a chance to reach out to Mina. Echoes of sympathy pain roll through my chest, making me wince. She's too weary to speak, but I recognize the look in her tear-filled eyes. It's the same combination of longing, fear, and relief I'm experiencing.

Hi.

The single word, silent greeting almost makes me cry, as does the sight of blood on her chin. Someone wiped most of the blood away, but there's still a spot just below her chin. I wish I could will Paige and Roy away. Not microjumping to Mina's side consumes my willpower.

"I'm almost suspicious of my good fortune," Paige says, "but that dumb expression you're wearing explains a lot." She rolls her eyes and reaches for Mina's right hand.

The sound of metal cuffs clicking into place rings out loudly.

Spirit cuffs.

The pain in my chest spikes as I finally identify the object Paige wields.

Mina's muffled cry slices straight to my core.

Paige loops the other end of the spirit cuffs to her left wrist and snaps it into place.

The pain cuts off.

Before I can work out what happened, Paige picks up

Mina's right hand and locks her attention on me.

"I'm going to make this very easy for you to understand, Allister," says Paige. Her legs cross as she gracefully lowers herself to a seat beside Mina. My friend's hand now rests in Paige's lap. "Mina took the liberty of connecting us so I couldn't teleport away and bring back hostages. You've been kind enough to furnish me with one anyway." She gives Roy a friendly nod.

He stares at her stonily.

I grit my teeth to endure the mock sympathy in Paige's voice. Clearing my throat, I make my pitch.

"Let me take her place." Even though Paige will never go for it, I'm shocked at how much I wish she would. "I'll take Spirit's Bane from Mina and go with you."

Paige chuckles.

"That's sweet of you, but I have other plans for you," says Paige. She lifts Mina's hand to focus my attention where she wants it. "Than will be joining us shortly. He'll bring us another set of spirit cuffs. I was going to use the threat against you to get dear Mina to accept her bonds with grace, but this works out better."

"Who's Than?" I ask, using the question to distract myself.

"That's right. I forgot. You would call him Abdon." Paige says, feigning surprise.

The revelation settles in my gut like a punch. Denials spring to mind even as my heart accepts the truth. Abdon acquitted himself well during the fight for the Academy, but now that I know, I realize I detected his presence at Mina's safehouse. He must have confronted her there.

"Anyway, when he arrives, I expect you to submit yourself to the spirit cuffs without a fuss." Paige's lightly delivered statement sticks sharp claws into me. "You see, I am currently holding the effects at bay, so Mina won't be forced into spirit form. If you defy me, I will stop intervening."

To prove her point, Paige does exactly that for three seconds.

Mina only groans, but I receive an echo and know she's contending with the evil pendant.

"Stop!" I don't have to pretend to beg.

135

Wearing spirit cuffs wasn't part of my plan, but I have no choice. The rational part of me knows Paige could torture Mina after I submit, but I need to believe she's not senselessly evil.

Paige's grimly triumphant expression tells me she knows I'm completely at her mercy.

Chapter 23:
You Can Change

Case Report #: MN-125
Case Agents: Master Blaz and Mistress Codee
Guardian: Mina Nadir

Allister has lousy timing. I'm overwhelmingly glad to see him, but the feeling comes with a heavy sense of guilt and fear. He came for me. He'll stay for me, even if I tell him to go. I know because I would stay for him. I don't know why he brought a human with him, but my connection to Allister makes me feel like I already know Roy Santori. Trusting my friend has a reason for bringing the human, I silently reach out and place a blessing upon Roy. It's not much protection, but it should keep demons from possessing him.

Paige continues to hold Spirit's Bane at bay for me while she gives Allister a chance to ponder his position.

It's not good for either of them.

Pain on its own is not a bad thing. By design, it declares that something needs to be fixed. Like so many of the Rebel's followers, Paige wields pain as a weapon. The act itself carries a darkness that infects the soul.

"This … is enough." I mean that the hold Paige has on me will keep Allister compliant, but the effort to explain in full lies beyond me right now.

"I believe you," Paige says, "but this is about more than control. It's about proving a point." She addresses the first part to me before looking to Allister.

"What do you want me to say?" Allister's frustration makes his tone bitter.

"You could start by telling me I was right," says Paige with a shrug.

"Allister—" I begin.

Paige cuts me off with a shushing noise and squeezes the hand she holds.

"Leave the discussion to us," she urges.

Despite the futility, I want to tell Allister to go, but I'm distracted by Paige reaching over and gently rubbing a spot on my chin.

"You still have blood on you," she comments.

I want to tell her she can change, but I sense the timing for the reminder isn't quite right.

"If you put it there, I will make you pay," Allister declares.

"I didn't," Paige assures my friend. "What I told you before is true. That was done by Spirit's Bane. It's getting stronger."

"What's Spirit's Bane?" asks Roy.

Paige's head snaps in his direction. She stares at him for a long second before explaining.

"It's a device meant to keep angels in their mortal form until they can be killed."

Abdon appears before Roy can ask another question. The smile he gives Paige chills me. Her features harden. The air around us thickens with an unnatural white fog.

"We don't need the theatrics, Than," says Paige. "Get Allister in spirit cuffs and go wherever you were told to take him."

"And miss out on the glory of seeing the Dark Master?" asks Abdon, spreading his arms to present the fog. "I think not. I'm going with you."

The fog darkens and shifts until faint forms can be detected within. I can barely focus on their exchange. My mind fixates on the prospect of meeting Lucifer again.

"That wasn't the plan." Paige's voice is tight with irritation.

"It was always my plan," Abdon says. He shakes his shoulders, puffs out his chest, and adjusts his tone to something near a whine. "Besides, what does it matter? I trust my demons to do their jobs without me for a few hours. I deserve this."

I fully expect him to stamp a foot, but he does not.

"You deserve *this*," Allister says darkly. He points Tyre at Abdon.

I didn't even see him draw the spirit sword.

Paige glances between the two before giving me an uncertain look. She wants to leap up and confront Abdon but doing so will divert attention away from shutting down Spirit's Bane.

"I can stand," I whisper, understanding her need to not face Abdon from the ground. The pain-free moments in Allister's presence have restored some of my strength.

Nodding, Paige stands and helps me up. My legs tremble but hold. Paige releases my hand and turns me until her left wrist, which is still attached to my right one, loops around my waist so she can support me.

Allister faces Abdon. They both hold spirit swords and stand roughly twenty feet apart. Roy stands a few feet beyond Allister. The human looks remarkably relaxed given the fact that he's surrounded by demons, two angels, and two dark angels.

"Than, do your job," says Paige. "Allister, don't give him any trouble."

Nobody moves.

Paige sighs.

"Convince him." Paige mutters the instruction into my right ear. She doesn't bother uttering a threat, but an unspoken one hangs in the air around us.

She means Allister, but my thoughts turn to Abdon. He brims with pride and defiance. The smallest push will turn him against Paige, but if I let that happen, their conflict could easily consume the rest of us.

Roy would die.

"Than." His name sounds strange on my lips. Praying for wisdom and truth to fill me, I pause until he reluctantly meets my gaze. "Your chosen name means 'brilliant' and 'death,' but I know you as Abdon, which means 'servant.'"

"What's your point?" Abdon's tone is guarded.

The temptation to spark a fight tugs at my spirit.

"The glory you seek is not found here," I answer. "It may seem real, but it is hollow." A flash of insight strikes me. He's only ever used a fraction of his abilities in Hadeon's service. My heart aches for Abdon. He seeks approval because he knows the value of encouragement. I want him to find his true purpose and follow it. "Hadeon and Lucifer cannot give you peace, but if you wish to serve them, obey their commands."

Allister's expression declares his alarm. I feel him desperately reaching out for me. Tentatively, I open my spirit to him. After purposefully shutting him out for so long, I expect the connection to feel strange, but instead, I'm filled with joy, wonder, and peace. Spirit's Bane responds with a sharp ache, but it's overwhelmed by Allister's presence.

Brief though those moments were, I wouldn't trade them for anything.

At first, Allister acts like an overbearing parent, examining every part of me for injury. Then, his protective instincts kick in and grip Spirit's Bane. I momentarily fight him over the idea of transferring the weapon to him. The offer touches me and renews my resolve to see this through.

We think forward the situation together. If we fight, Roy will likely die. That part, I knew. If we stall too long, Hadeon or Lucifer will grow impatient. That scenario doesn't end well either. Attempting to talk to Abdon will set him against Paige, leading to violence. There's a very slim chance Paige may help us eventually, but she's not ready yet. For that to work, we need her to continue feeling in control. The impression we need to build requires surrender. Allister and I draw the counterintuitive conclusion together.

We must part ways for now.

Allister doesn't like the thought, but he agrees.

Lacking time for finesse, I quickly renew the connection between our spirits, thank Allister for his love and trust, and shut him out again.

Paige tightens her grip on me, but Allister addresses Abdon before she can ask what I've done.

"I will go with you, if you release Roy," he says.

Abdon studies his sword thoughtfully.

"I'd rather kill him," he mutters.

The fog of demons behind Roy thickens and forces him to step toward Abdon. Tendrils of fog wrap around Roy's arms and legs, binding him. He's still unnaturally calm, and this time, I sense Allister channeling the peace through Empathy.

"Pretty sure Hadeon would call that a stupid waste," Allister says. "When that lands you on his bad side, I'm going to say: 'I told you so.'"

"You may be right," Abdon admits. He tosses a pair of spirit cuffs to Allister. "Put those on, and I'll put off his execution … for now."

A shudder runs through me. I think we've selected the right path forward, but Abdon could still snap any second.

"You're playing dangerous games," Paige whispers to me. "I don't know what they are but stop it." Her suspicious tone tells me she has a guess.

"I wish it were a game," I say, keeping my voice soft, "but your soul is worth so much more. No matter what happens, remember, you have a choice. You can change."

Allister and Abdon are too absorbed with their standoff to mind us, but these words aren't only meant for Paige.

"Stop trying to save me," she snaps.

Her exasperation gives me hope.

"Save your strength for yourself," says Paige. "You're going to need it." She tries to sound firm and harsh, but I still detect distinct notes of weariness.

By this time, Allister has fully accepted the spirit cuffs. They hold his wrists together in front of his body.

Abdon's demons cheer as he uses the cuffs to pull Allister in his direction.

I flinch, expecting Abdon to stab my friend.

At the last instant, Allister's body halts just before meeting the outstretched blade. Slowly, Abdon lowers the sword. Next, the sword disappears, and Abdon drives a fist into Allister's jaw, knocking him back a step. He follows the blow with two more quick strikes before Roy jumps in front of Allister and catches the third punch with both hands. The force knocks his hands back into his chest, and he hits the hard ground gasping for breath.

Abdon's eyes blaze with fury.

"Never get in my way!" he shouts.

Roy shuts his eyes and goes still.

I try to go to him, but Paige holds me fast.

Allister battles his spirit cuffs to get to Roy, but the demons haul him back several steps.

"Let me save him," he demands.

"No," says Abdon.

"Not your call," Paige counters. "Those are my cuffs." She waves, overriding the spirit cuffs holding my friend.

The silver chains drop off his wrists.

Abdon trembles with rage.

I delve deep into spirit to reach out to Abdon with a sense of peace. To my surprise, I feel Paige joining the work.

"Make it quick, Allister," says Paige. "I want you back in those cuffs soon."

Allister nods, microjumps to Roy's side, and places his left hand over the man's chest. A tense moment passes before the human gasps and falls into a coughing fit. When he finishes the healing work, Allister returns to the cuffs and puts them on again.

"Why did you do that?" Abdon's anger renders the question raggedly.

I can't tell if the question is meant for Allister or Paige, but she answers first.

"Follow your orders," says Paige. "We need to separate them quickly. The human is no good to you dead. Take him with you as an extra measure of control over Allister. Do this, and I will tell Lord Hadeon of your good work today."

Abdon shakes his head once.

"Words mean little," he says. "I will show the Dark Master what I can do in person."

"At least make your delivery first," Paige argues.

After careful consideration, Abdon agrees to this plan. Relief and fear shoot through me. Allister's chances of escaping his prison increase if Abdon follows us, but I do not look forward to meeting the Rebel again. Our last encounter was unpleasant, and surely, Hadeon will be waiting as well, longing to see how I've fared against Spirit's Bane.

"Where shall I meet you?" asks Abdon.

"Reach out to me after you've completed your task," answers Paige. "I will give you the location then." She nods to Allister. "He'd better be secure before you act upon that knowledge."

Allister will find us.

I think the words as a fervent wish and a solemn promise.

Chapter 24:
Not Compatible

Dear Master,

My informants in both legions report success. We have the Kindred Spirit Pair in custody and under some semblance of control. They should be on their way to the containment sites shortly. Than will take the boy to an old mine in Eastern Siberia, and Daeva will escort the girl to the abandoned town of Craco in Italy. We have a third location—Pripyat—ready in the Ukraine for Mina. There's still excess radiation there from the Chernobyl incident that may further weaken her mortal form.

Deimos is handling the details at each site, and then, he will await further instructions in the Ukraine. We've decided to place Aderes at the boy's location and Lady Codee at the girl's location. Deimos said you wish to participate in breaking Mina. We would be honored to have you.

I will meet you there as soon as I check in with Than.

He's a good agent, but his ego tends to be fragile. If I ignore him, he will mentally magnify the slight into a much greater offense. Over time, that will allow resentment to fester in him.

You asked me to describe my thoughts on breaking the Kindred Spirit Bond, so I will do so soon. I apologize for not doing so at first, but I wanted to present my current thoughts on what to do with the bond once we have it.

The original plan involved repurposing the bond for Than and Daeva, but I am having doubts about that plan. The few exchanges I've witnessed tell me they are not compatible. He excels as a spymaster and manages his legions like few others, but that deep jealous streak may soon become more than a nuisance. Daeva has the opposite problem. She relies very heavily upon her own skills rather than inspiring those under her command.

Than's information is correct, but I do not believe he reports these things with pure intentions. I can confirm that we lost contact with Daeva for several hours. Despite repeated reminders to keep her support close, she often improvises. Her record of success is indisputable, but I am not comfortable leaving her alone with the girl for any meaningful length of time. Mina can be very persuasive. It's highly unlikely Daeva will waver, but I would rather not tempt her unnecessarily.

They are not going to like it, but I wish to send Daeva and Than on important missions elsewhere while we work on the Kindred Spirit Pair. They have achieved their objectives and deserve to share in the glory, but their lengthy missions have also placed them in positions that compromise their consciences. Given that last report from Than's minions, Daeva seems to respect the girl. That could be trouble for us later. A direct order from you will be much harder for them to ignore than one from me, but I will try to persuade them myself first.

Having Than and Daeva switch targets would do little good. Than may be even more susceptible to the girl's message of a second chance to bend the knee to their so-called Glorious King. The desperate need for approval is Than's one true flaw.

Thus ends my long-winded account of the problems with my original plan.

Do you think we could re-establish the bond between Mina and Deimos? The fact that he fathered the form that would have belonged to the girl connects them, but the only other bond we've dealt with recently has been between two angels of complementary Gifts and compatible dispositions.

We could also turn Aderes. Her lack of experience should work in our favor. She might pair well with Allister once Mina is gone, but I think it might be better to start fresh if we go with her. Than will desire the honor, but honestly, I believe either of Aderes's natural friends, Adelmo or Osmund, would be better suited.

Since we have full control over Josiah's spirit, we might even be able to give the bond back to him and Elizabeth Codee, but that would require recovering his mortal form.

Each scenario assumes we have the Kindred Spirit Bond, which is not the case yet. That will change shortly.

Operatives at both containment sites have instructions on how to proceed with the proposals to dissolve the bond. It's difficult to predict who will fold first. If I had to place odds at this moment, I would say Allister is the more likely candidate. We may need to do nothing more but let Spirit's Bane torment the girl and offer to end it upon his cooperation.

As planned, the chase has worn down the girl's body, but her will to resist remains largely untouched. The previously described strategy might work here. To that end, we may get the best results from Mina by exerting pressure on Allister and Lady Codee. After the months of living with Spirit's Bane, I doubt physical pain will move the girl much.

If the first phase doesn't work, we could extend the misfortune to the school Mina guarded for a few months. Watching her charges come under severe spiritual attack will hit her hard. Knowing she can stop it could be her breaking point. There's work aplenty on Earth. Shifting operations one way or the other will have little overall impact upon the long-term plans.

Everything we do is for your glory.

If there is time, I would like to hear your thoughts on these matters. I look forward to working alongside you.

Your devoted servant,

Hadeon

***

Dear Than,

I am aware of your desire to quickly wrap up your duties with the boy and come witness the Master's work with the girl.

I advise against such a decision.

You control most of the demons at the Siberian containment site. They deserve your attention and skillful leadership. You must convince the boy to give up his portion of the Kindred Spirit Bond.

Do not fail me.

I'm told by the Dark Master himself that if your performance proves worthy, he will consider giving you another important task and much more power. He may decide to do so anyway based upon your success thus far, but if I tell him you disobeyed a direct order, those prospects will disappear.

I do not want to see you until you have succeeded.

Is anything I've said unclear?

Hadeon, Servant of the Dark Master,

Director of Operations

***

Dear Daeva,

I can always trust you to get the job done, but you continue to impress me. I appreciate the subtle ways you've bonded with the girl. If there's any chance she can be turned, it will exist because of your hard work. That said, it's time you moved on to a new assignment. Once

147

you safely deliver the girl to me, I will give you the location where Than took the boy. Go there and help him make the boy submit.

Know that I trust you but not the girl. She is devious and skilled at manipulation. She will not hesitate to lie to you.

The Dark Master has received my report on your excellent work. In fact, he should be present when you arrive with the girl. If he comes up with an assignment and gives it to you directly, of course, it will supersede mine. Should that happen, please let me know so I can get Than proper support from elsewhere as soon as possible.

He will resent your presence unless you convince him you understand your role there is that of support. While technically true, I am also relying heavily upon you to keep Than focused on the goal. I fear his impatience will cause his work to suffer.

Thank you for your service.
Hadeon, Servant of the Dark Master,
Director of Operations

Part 4:
Prisoners

Chapter 25:
In a Hurry

Case Report #: AK-125
Case Agent: Mistress Adira Clarimond
Guardian: Allister Knight

Once Paige and Mina disappear, I help Roy to his feet. The spirit cuffs make supporting him awkward. He's still weak from Abdon's chest punch. The blow had crushed Roy's sternum back into his heart and lungs, causing several ribs to break. One rib even pierced the left lung. I'd be surprised if he didn't technically die for a short time. The internal bleeding was extensive. Normally, I wouldn't be able to heal damage like that quickly, but Mina's presence made it possible.

She's been gone almost a minute, and I miss her already. I'm certain I'll see her shortly, but the endless possibilities for bad things that could happen to her before then terrify me. The brief time we had together showed me that her spirit's still strong, but her mortal form is fading. If we can't destroy Spirit's Bane soon, Mina will die.

"She won't suffer long," Abdon says. His tone is brisk and factual. He places a hand on my left arm and Roy's right arm.

"If that's supposed to be comforting, you're terrible at this," I say, glaring at him.

Abdon shrugs and teleports us somewhere.

The wide-open spaces and fresh air disappear. We arrive

150

in a well-lit underground cavern. Instinctively, I check for our location to make sure we're still on Earth.

The words **Eastern Siberia, Russia** cross my mind.

It's far from the United States of America, but at least, Roy should be able to breathe. Since Abdon could have taken us to one of a few hundred thousand planets in this galaxy alone, most of which aren't suitable for human life, I'm grateful for the small favor.

"Take it as you will," Abdon comments. He drops his hold on us and steps back. "I don't care."

Beside me, Roy shivers.

"Do you have a coat or a blanket for him?" I ask Abdon.

He nods toward a spot above and behind me. I turn in time to see the shadows shifting.

Demons. Wonderful.

Now that I pause to think, I realize the air reeks of them.

Roy's eyes bulge, confirming the bad feeling.

I don't need to see in spirit form to know we're surrounded.

"Settle in, human. I'll have someone bring you a blanket soon," says Abdon. He gestures for Roy to be seated on an old wooden crate.

I notice that without Paige around, he's more direct. And he preens less. I wonder how I've missed his behavior before.

Has he always tried to impress her?

Shaking my head to dislodge the thought, I watch as a man jogs over to us holding several blankets. Without meeting our eyes, he throws his cargo at Roy, ducks his head, and hurries away, muttering to himself.

Pulling one blanket around his shoulders and another across his lap, Roy sits on the crate and leans back against the wall.

He should be safe for the moment, leaving me enough capacity to indulge in anger over the slave. He wears no physical chains, but a peek into the spirit realm shows several dozen demons. Most are inside him, but some cling to his back and shoulders like barnacles. As I suspected, the rest of the room also teems with dark spirits, both corrupted angels in spirit form and natural demons.

"Release that man," I demand.

Abdon shoots me a disgusted look and snaps his fingers.

The spirit cuffs pull me forward and down until I'm kneeling before him.

"I don't have time for your bleeding-heart nonsense," says Abdon. "I need to be elsewhere, but before I get to go there, I need you to release your hold on the Kindred Spirit Bond." He looks at me expectantly.

I stare up at him blankly.

Abdon's gaze hardens, and his hands form fists.

"Now, Allister," he growls. "You have three seconds to agree before I off your human friend and let my legion rip the soul out of your sweet little angel friend."

"Mina's beyond your reach," I say.

Confusion crosses Abdon's face. It's followed quickly by surprise and several other emotions, most of which are some form of weariness or frustration. He has the spirit cuffs haul me upright again and spirit flashes us across the large cavern.

Moving through multiple demons puts an uneasy feeling deep in my gut.

"I wasn't referring to Mina," says Abdon. "The Dark Master will deal with her."

Unnatural white fog surrounds us, but it rolls back, revealing a small, still form lying on the ground. Her back faces me, but the long light brown hair and thin frame are familiar.

"Show him," Abdon orders.

Tendrils form out of the fog. They wind around the figure's limbs and wrap around her core before pulling her up and turning her around. It looks like a rag doll being animated. The angel's head flops to the side until another strand of fog twines around her neck and forces her head up. Dirt covers her face. She's obviously unconscious. Loose strands of hair further obscure her features, but I recognize her anyway.

It's Aderes.

"Bring her," says Abdon.

Next instant, we're back by Roy along with Aderes. The demon fog drops her before Roy's crate. Leaping up, he wraps her in the blanket he'd had across his lap and carefully picks her up.

Anger makes my blood run hot. I open my mouth to demand what they did to her, but Abdon speaks first.

"There are thousands of lives I can threaten besides these two." Abdon glances about, issuing silent orders.

Soon, a cage made of demons in their creepy fog form springs up around Roy and Aderes.

"Normally, I'd enjoy breaking you properly, but I'm in a hurry," Abdon continues. "I need that bond, and I need it now."

I stare at him, still confused.

"What do you want with a Kindred Spirit Bond?" I wonder.

"Not for you to know," Abdon says. "What's your decision?"

His answer tells me he has no clue what his masters intend to do with what they seek. I never thought the bond might be a tangible thing that could be transferred, but I lack time to think on the matter properly. I barely have time for one disturbing thought.

If we lose the bond, what will change for Mina and me?

"I'm not trying to be stubborn." I drag the sentence out. "As far as I know, I've always had this special connection to Mina, but I'd never considered it something to be held on to or laid down. I don't know how to give you what you want."

"Lucky for you then that I got this out of the Grand Library," Abdon says.

He reaches into the Veil that stands between worlds and pulls out a book. It's called *The Essential Guide to Making the Most of the Kindred Spirit Connection*.

"I've marked the relevant passage," says Abdon. "Read this, follow the instructions, and it'll be done."

My heart beats painfully inside me. I don't think this is going to unfold as Abdon would like, but for now, I need to pretend to cooperate.

Roy's trying to catch my attention, but I ignore him. It's not time to enact our crazy plan yet, and I don't want to give anything away by acting suspicious. We need to get Abdon to reveal where they've taken Mina. Trying to locate her by Trace alone will take too long. I might be able to find Paige again, but there's no guarantee that she's still with Mina.

Abdon braces the book against his forearms to hold it steady while I read over the section he has marked.

***

Kindred Spirit Bonds are a rare gift from our Glorious King. They magnify the Gifts given to both parties and draw the bound souls together by an unbreakable cord. However, like any gift, the bond can be rejected.

Relationships change. If two souls connected by a Kindred Spirit Bond wish to be free of each other, they may dissolve the bond permanently by sending a heartfelt petition of the rejection to the King. His love is perfect. He will never force his servants to bear such a blessing unwillingly.

Take heed: If done improperly, the dissolution of a Kindred Spirit Bond can do great harm to both persons. Those considering such a weighty matter should proceed with caution.

If the dissolution goes smoothly, leaving the bond intact, the King may bestow it upon two others. If it breaks, He will craft a new one so that every generation will be led by a committed pair of worthy angels.

The enemy jealously yearns for a gift like the Kindred Spirit Bond but take heart. What you have cannot be stolen. Only the pure of heart may bear the bond to good effect.

***

I stop reading and meet Abdon's expectant gaze.

"Did you read the whole thing?" I ask. If he had, we wouldn't be having this conversation, but I want to hear his thoughts. "The bond won't work properly if it's stolen."

"It's not going to be stolen," Abdon argues. "You're going to release it willingly."

"I can't," I say, really wishing I could lie about that. "It

154

would mean rejecting Mina."

"She'll be dead soon anyway," Abdon says. "Your connection is probably all that's keeping her alive and in pain now. Releasing her would be a kindness."

His words force me to consider the awful possibility.

"Don't listen to that rubbish," Roy says. "He knows nothin' more than you or I do."

"Quiet!" Abdon commands. He turns and focuses his contempt on Roy. "Humans are a blight upon the Earth. I look forward to the day my Master gives me leave to destroy your kind."

Several demons become like living shadows and encircle Roy's neck until his breathing turns labored. They likely can't kill him directly, but they can certainly hold him still long enough for Abdon to do so by staying in human form.

Abdon waves a hand to keep the demons from choking Roy further.

"For now, hold your peace and play your part as a silent hostage," says Abdon. "If Allister doesn't waste any more of my time, I might dump you back wherever you came from before going to meet my Master."

The awe in his voice when he speaks of Satan moves me. Mina was right. He's seeking after hollow glory, but what he really needs is peace and acceptance. For the first time in a while, I don't argue with the Empathy driven logic. Instead, I reach out with my spirit and offer Abdon quiet comfort. His shoulders relax, but then, his whole body goes rigid.

"What are you doing?" he asks.

"Not sure," I murmur, still working. His spirit feels fractured and defeated. I'm tempted to leave the spirit as I found it because repairing the damage might make Abdon more of a tyrant.

Love as our King loves. Heal what is broken.

The reminder sounds like it's from Mina.

"Fixing what is broken," I say, starting to knit the spirit pieces back together.

"No." Abdon withdraws from my spirit touch abruptly. "The way of light is a lie. I deserve power and glory, and your King won't give it to me. Nobody will give it to me." He draws a dagger from the Veil and studies the shiny surface. "I will earn it."

Suddenly, the spirit cuffs cast me to my knees again.

Abdon places the dagger on my right shoulder like one giving a blessing.

"You've got a strong spirit," he says, "but you have no idea how long and hard I've worked to get where I am. You will give me what the Master wants or suffer first and then surrender. Choose wisely because I'm out of patience."

Chapter 26:
My Fight

Case Report #: MN-126
Case Agents: Master Blaz and Mistress Codee
Guardian: Mina Nadir

By the time Paige teleports us to our new destination, I'm strong enough to stand up on my own. The reprieve from pain has allowed me to recover much of the strength spent running away. I expect Paige to withdraw from the spirit cuffs, but she stays connected and maintains her supportive hold on me. In fact, her grip tightens as we absorb the surroundings.

Paige's heartbeats have quickened. She reaches out in spirit, but I don't know what she's searching for.

We're in an old abandoned church. Not much distinguishes it from any other crumbling ruin, but Allister's ability to manipulate time manifests in a strange new way. I suddenly see into the church's past from when the first stone was laid until an earthquake cracked the foundation in several places. Joy and sorrow mingle in me as the history runs through me like water.

We're not alone.

Every particle of dust feels tainted. This place hosts a lot of demons. Even without tuning my eyes and ears to the spirit realm, I sense the malicious glee in the air.

Two figures materialize before us. Both handsome men

wear clean suits. Hadeon—the tall, blond man on the left from my perspective—wears a black suit with a red rose pinned near his heart. The Prince of Darkness—the dark-haired man on the right—wears a charcoal gray suit with a dark blue tie. Their features are slightly different than at our last meeting, but I think that's because they have aged their projections to be late thirties and early forties, rather than mid-twenties and early thirties, respectively.

"Well done, Daeva," says the Prince of Darkness. His rich voice rolls out smoothly, inviting listeners to let down their guard. "Lord Hadeon has spoken very highly of your work. I am pleased to see that his praise is merited."

"Thank you, Master," Paige answers.

She kneels beside me, bows her head to her chest, and tugs on my right hand, indicating that I should join her.

I stay on my feet and watch the pair warily.

A predatory smile crosses Lucifer's features. Once again, his thick, dark hair rises back from his forehead in several waves. His eyes are pale blue, almost gray this time.

"You are most welcome as well, Mina," he says. "I apologize for the lacking décor, but after the last incident went awry, I decided to sacrifice beauty for security. I hope you understand. Are you ready to die this time?"

"My fate isn't yours to decide," I remind him.

Lucifer chuckles.

"I forgot how calm and brave you could be," he comments. "I hope you'll refuse me when I ask nicely for the Kindred Spirit Bond because it will be so much fun taking it from you."

"It can't be stolen," I say. I'd meant to say something else, but the words that come out fill me, leaving room for nothing else.

"Give me control of the spirit cuffs, and you may go to your next assignment." The statement to Paige comes from Hadeon.

Paige hesitates. Her grip on my hand tightens. Without lifting her head, she directs her response evenly to both demons.

"I would like to stay with her and see this through."

"That's not—"

Lucifer raises a manicured hand, cutting off Hadeon's protest.

"Why? What is her fate to you?" asks Lucifer. He keeps his tone light and curious as he slowly approaches us, but there's malice in the undercurrents.

I want to warn Paige not to answer, but power radiating from the Prince of Darkness surrounds us. It's like a corrupted version of Empathy, reaching out and demanding a response.

"She's my responsibility," Paige whispers.

"Is that all?" Lucifer queries cheerfully. Placing his left hand on Paige's head, he continues, "Very well then. I relieve you of that responsibility."

A shock surges down through her skull and courses throughout her body instantly. Her cry reaches my ears the same moment as our hands are blasted apart, snapping the metal cuffs. The energy throws me into the left wall. I don't even get a chance to brace before striking the stone wall and landing on my back. I slip into twilight state to assess the damage, but before I can get much information, I'm compelled into full spirit. Searing pain from Spirit's Bane forces me back into human form.

The cycle of transformations continues three more times in quick succession. When I'm finally allowed to stay in my mortal state, I don't bother rising. I've landed sideways.

But Lucifer's not done his demonstration.

The spirit cuffs form fresh bindings for my wrists, snap together tightly, and drag me back to the spot where I started. I'm left on the floor facing my captors.

I stare up at Paige who stands directly in front of Lucifer, looking conflicted. She must have given him some control over the spirit cuffs, but I don't think she's completely surrendered them yet.

"Look long and think hard," instructs Lucifer. He circles around to Paige's other side. "That is the face of our enemy. She may look innocent, but she serves a charlatan. Do you wish to cast your lot with them?"

"Master, Daeva has proven herself many times over," says Hadeon. "Good servants are hard to find. Perhaps we should—"

"Test her," Lucifer finishes. "Splendid idea."

159

He takes a small switchblade from his breast pocket and slides the blade out.

"This is coated with a synthetic nerve agent," explains Lucifer. "Kill her and move us one step closer to victory."

"Master, we need the bond first," says Hadeon.

"It will be free once she's dead," Lucifer assures Hadeon with a shrug.

"This isn't necessary," Hadeon presses.

"I think it is." Lucifer's voice turns deadly calm, warning Hadeon against further discussion.

Before Lucifer can hand Paige the switchblade, she disappears.

Desperately, I try to sever the tie I created between our spirits back in the desert, but I'm not quick enough.

Paige reappears and stands above me, looking calmer than before.

Hadeon's posture has stiffened.

I finally succeed in severing the connection to Paige.

"You can leave now," I say to her.

"No, she can't," counters Lucifer. "You've corrupted her."

"Please go," I beg Paige. I don't have the energy to think forward her future, but Lucifer's intent seems abundantly clear.

"Why are you doing this?" Hadeon asks. "Daeva has been ours since infancy."

"This was an interesting experiment while it lasted, I'll give you that," says Lucifer. He lets his gaze linger on Paige while addressing Hadeon. "But there's too much light in her. Don't you sense it? You failed to drive it out when you had the chance. This act will make her ours forever or expose her as a traitor. Either way, we'll know the truth soon."

With Lucifer's attention focused on Paige, I recover enough strength to try something new. I let Allister's Gift for controlling time flow through me again. Concentrating, I focus the Gift on Paige and watch the changes she's undergone over time in rapid succession. Most of the images show her training or answering to Hadeon. Several show her killing in his name. They're not clear pictures as they're pieced together memories formed by her spirit rather than her mind, but the earliest one shows me a smiling woman with long, flowing gold hair. I don't recognize her, but I feel like I should.

Paige starts to sweat as she fights to free herself from Lucifer's invisible hold. Suddenly, she stops struggling and looks down at me.

"I'm sorry," she murmurs. Her voice sounds dead. "This is who I'm meant to be."

I don't believe her.

Slowly, as if in a trance, Paige walks over to Lucifer who carefully hands her the switchblade.

Suddenly, she's gone again and back a few seconds after her disappearance, this time without the weapon.

The chains around my wrists have changed.

They're no longer spirit cuffs, only pieces of metal.

"Foolish, child," scolds Lucifer. He waves his hand dramatically and the switchblade reappears. He tucks it away. "Did you really think that would work?"

"It served its purpose," Paige replies calmly.

This is my fight.

I'm not sure what to make of Paige's thought to me.

"Hadeon, bind her," Lucifer orders.

Shaking his head in frustration, Hadeon snaps the fingers of his right hand. Silver chains appear and wrap tightly around Paige. A second later, they fall away. Hadeon looks confused, but Lucifer only smiles and offers Paige mocking applause.

The spirit cuffs Paige took from me and wore temporarily to prevent Hadeon's set from controlling her fall away and return to me. However, instead of confining me, they settle around my wrist manacles and subtly destabilize the metal.

Demons bleed from the air and surround Paige in a thick gray cloud, holding her tight and lifting her a few inches off the ground.

"I didn't want it to come to this," Hadeon laments.

"Cheer up," says Lucifer. "Today, we will right two mistakes and claim a Kindred Spirit Bond."

He raises both hands slowly.

"I'm tired of hiding in the shadows," comments Lucifer. "And so it appears are my many followers."

Thousands of eyes appear in the air above and around us.

Julie C. Gilbert

Only a small area above our group remains clear of demons.

Chapter 27:
Holy Host

Case Report #: AK-126
Case Agent: Mistress Adira Clarimond
Guardian: Allister Knight

I should feel more fear, but instead, I pity Abdon. He doesn't even realize how much the hatred twisting his soul burdens him. The rage coursing through him brings his dagger in contact with my neck, opening a shallow cut on the right side. Mina's healing Gift closes the wound, but the sting of it lingers.

"You are not evil, Abdon," I say, unsure where the words come from. They're certainly not the ones I intended to voice.

Wanting to prove me wrong, Abdon draws his dagger back and punches my face with his free hand.

The blow knocks me down sideways. I land awkwardly on my left arm and roll onto my back.

A muffled protest comes from Roy. I glance his way in time to see the slave who delivered the blanket stuff a dirty rag into Roy's mouth.

Aderes stirs.

I should get up and fight back, but something compels me to close my eyes and silently pray for Abdon.

A strangled cry that is half a sob rips itself from Abdon's throat.

Pain explodes in both shoulders as something lands hard across them.

My eyes snap open and fix on Abdon's face. His features have formed a blank mask.

"Still think I'm not evil?" The question hisses out on a wave of hot breath.

Slowly, he presses the dagger's blade into my left shoulder. I try to shift to spirit to avoid the attack, but the spirit cuffs stop me. Comfort and peace wrap around me even as the sharp pain intensifies. I grit my teeth to hold in a cry. Once I've had a chance to adjust to the discomfort, I draw a shaky breath.

"It's not my claim," I tell Abdon.

"Whose then?" he demands, withdrawing the dagger.

My shoulder muscles start to heal, but the shirt's still torn and covered in blood.

"The King," answers Aderes. She stands beside Roy who still occupies the wooden crate. They're about the same height with him seated and her standing tall.

I'm relieved to see the air around her shimmer, indicating that she's shielding herself.

"You're supposed to be unconscious," Abdon mutters. He narrows his eyes accusingly at Aderes.

"Allister's presence must have enhanced my healing abilities," she says with a shrug.

Abdon grunts.

"No matter," he says. "I have plenty of normal hostages." Abdon stares at Aderes and me in turn. "If either of you try anything, I'll have my slaves destroy the entire town of Mirny and its 45,000 souls."

"You do not have the weapons to accomplish this," says Aderes.

"This used to be a diamond mine," Abdon explains. "It's obviously abandoned now, but they dug a lot of tunnels in the hopes of expanding. All I need to do is collapse the right ones and the entire town will disappear into a sinkhole."

"But you don't want to do that," I say, picking up on the reluctance in his tone.

Abdon grips a section of my shirt in his left fist.

"What I want to do is go meet the Dark Master," he says slowly. "But I need your bond first. It's a simple exchange: many lives for one. Doesn't that appeal to your pathetic heroic nature?"

"It's not my life to bargain with," I remind him.

"We are subjects of the King," says Aderes. "As are you. Do you not hear his call to stop rebelling?"

I don't hear Abdon's response, for suddenly, Paige appears in my mind and rapidly fills it with images. The first is a pair of hands cupped around a white dove. I believe it's a sign of peace. The next two show places, a beautiful island and crumbling stone ruins on a hillside. Don't know their significance, but I'm guessing it has something to do with the fourth image, which consists of a series of numbers and symbols. The fifth gives me a glimpse of Mina. The sixth features two hands clasped together in friendship. The seventh and last shows me Paige kneeling with her head bowed, weeping.

A series of impatient slaps brings my attention back to the current situation.

"What happened?" asks Abdon. "What did you see?"

"I'm not sure," I answer.

The images were clear enough, but their implications remain a mystery.

Are they genuine or not?

It could be a trap. Paige never struck me as being overly fond of traps, but she's done devious things. Her Master really enjoys toying with lives. He might prompt her to such actions. Instinct tells me to trust the images, but I wish I had a few hours to analyze them properly.

The speed with which I received the missives tells me I'm out of time.

Glancing at Roy, I nod almost imperceptibly.

He leans back against the wall and shuts his eyes.

The plan is in motion.

I shift my left shoulder to see if the healing has completed. A twinge indicates that the work is almost done but not quite there yet.

"When we defeat you, remember that our King is merciful. Your master is not," I say. A heaviness drops over my heart. "But the more you harden your heart, the further you move from true light and life."

Anger clouds Abdon's expression as he jabs the dagger at my left shoulder again.

Instead of sinking through flesh, the weapon crashes hard into an invisible shield, sending up sparks of light.

"That's impossible," Abdon whispers. He gapes down at his dagger like it betrayed him. "Your Gifts don't cover shields."

"Mine do," Aderes says. Suddenly, she flips to spirit and magnifies her presence.

The cage of demons scatters with a chorus of soul-chilling screams.

Light shoots out of Roy in nearly every direction.

My spirit leaps with joy, greeting the newcomers.

As instructed, Roy keeps his eyes clenched shut to preserve his vision.

The spirit cuffs tighten painfully as Abdon grows increasingly desperate.

Beams of light quickly fill every dark corner.

The clouds of demons roll back and bunch up in several areas.

One by one, the sections of light coalesce into an angel. Some I recognize, including Reena, Osmund, Adelmo, Jabir, Valen, and a handful who participated in the raid on Forsaken Island, but most I do not. Each stands ready with their weapon of choice.

"You can end this conflict before it begins," I say to Abdon.

"I'd rather fight," he answers.

I brace, but Abdon still surprises me.

I'm forced into spirit.

Abdon conjures a despair whip, fashions it into a pointed stake, and plunges the weapon into my chest. Crippling cold paralyzes me. My mind fills with terror and hopelessness. Knowing it's a lie does little to comfort me. I curl onto my side and grip the despair whip, trying to wrench it free.

New cords from the whip bind my hands, making them stiff with cold. I'm stuck in twilight state, feeling both the bone-shaking cold in my physical form and the spiritual poison.

A wordless cry for help rips my throat raw on its way out.

On every side, spirit weapons clash. I can't keep track of everything, but I'm relieved to see Reena staying near Roy. A few slaves bearing makeshift weapons stand several feet from him. They wear blank expressions because the demons controlling them are suddenly busy fighting my friends. Before I shift my attention away from Roy, I notice his lips moving. He must be praying.

A spark of hope returns and warmth blossoms in my chest. Soon, the feeling magnifies tenfold. The power flooding me disintegrates the despair whip. My initial cry dies away as the dust from the despair whip showers down around me.

Abdon conjures a sword and swings it at me.

I roll aside, but the strike never lands.

Jabir slides in front of me and knocks Abdon's sword to the right so the blow hits the dirt floor.

Aderes appears above my head and places her hands on my shoulders.

The feeling she sends me infuses every part of my body and spirit with hope, strength, peace, and determination.

Tyre appears in my right hand as my spirit armor forms on me. I release him and try to move the spirit cuffs through his blade.

Nothing happens.

It's disappointing but not surprising.

Next, I spread my presence into the armor, letting the shiny gold plates magnify the light.

Several nearby demons shriek with pain as the light stabs through them.

Abdon stands a few feet away. Hatred taints the aura around him, turning it red and black.

"Their deaths are your fault." His eyes pin the statement to me.

Suddenly, every human slave falls to the ground and convulses, making me think Abdon's somehow killing them. Then, a far-off explosion shakes the cavern.

I freeze time in the mortal world to give Valen and Osmund a chance to aid the humans.

"You're too late," Abdon taunts when he fights through the hold I have over time. "The ground will collapse."

We can help them or you, but not both.

Aderes's thought reaches out to me with an implied question.

Using feelings instead of words, I tell her to take Roy and stop whatever Abdon has set in motion.

The room feels emptier as the angels who traveled in with Roy and many of the demons leave to continue the battle elsewhere in the mine. Aderes seemed confident that our small force can win, but I cannot help them.

My fight is here.

Since Abdon still controls the spirit cuffs, many of my Gifts are inaccessible. I'm surprised I could even summon Tyre, and I suspect it was only possible because the appearance of more angels distracted Abdon.

He recovers his focus and remembers the power he wields over me. Contempt crosses his face as Abdon uses the cuffs to force me into human form.

Tyre slips back into the Veil.

I'm not sure what happens with my armor. I suspect when I turn back into spirit, it will be waiting for me.

Thick chains form around my body. The light from my presence dims. I want to fight the effects, but weariness sweeps over me.

Spirit cuffs can be broken. I've seen it done for Mina, but the last time, we had a whole host helping us. This time, I've sent the backup elsewhere.

You are not alone.

The strong voice comforts me, but it holds no other encouragements or answers.

Abdon stands over me.

"I can't kill you, but I can hurt you for every inconvenience." He kneels beside me and lowers his voice, changing tactics. "It's just us, Allister. You can stop fighting. Give me the bond. Why drag this out?"

"I won't betray Mina," I say, shaking my head.

Abdon punches me, shakes his hand, and makes a growling noise.

"Let me explain how this goes. Every time you say something stupid, I hit you," says Abdon. "When I'm tired of hitting you, I turn you to spirit and let the demons have you for a while. Then, you return to flesh and we start again. This could be a very long night, but you *will* give me what I want."

Chapter 28:
Like Old Times

Case Report #: MN-127
Case Agents: Master Blaz and Mistress Codee
Guardian: Mina Nadir

The chains binding my wrists crumble. The spirit cuffs that once created those chains finish their current task and disappear. Slowly, I push myself up to a sitting position. I should take the gift of freedom Paige has given me and teleport away, but I'm done running. I use the quiet moment to ask the King for the will to see this through. It would be so easy to give in and let the Prince of Darkness kill me, but that would let Spirit's Bane fall into their hands again. They would do this to somebody else, and the months of safeguarding the weapon would be completely wasted.

Hadeon stands off to the side sulking and quietly directing the demons in the room.

Lucifer looks irritated, but soon, his mocking smile returns.

"I'm surprised you're still here, though I shouldn't be," he says. "You can't abandon her." With a flourish, he conjures another set of spirit cuffs and tosses them toward me.

They land near my feet and glow bright orange.

"Don't!" Paige only gets out that one word, but it's enough to convey her wishes.

The demons holding Paige renew their efforts to subdue

her. The cloud disappears in favor of gray and black streams that bind her wrists and ankles. Several demons form into sharp spikes that congregate at her throat, forcing her head to tip up. Their meaning is clear. The rest create a misty cage around her to discourage a shift to spirit.

"Put those on and I'll introduce you to our other guest," says Lucifer.

My head hurts and my body aches with fatigue. I don't feel up to another round of dealing with spirit cuffs, but I must know who else needs protecting. I have escaped spirit cuffs before, but only with a lot of help from many other angels.

I am with you, and I am enough.

The thought from my King dispels some of my fears.

Adjusting my position so that I'm kneeling, I bow my head and hold my hands out, palms up. The spirit cuffs snap into place and pull my wrists together.

I brace, knowing Lucifer will flaunt the control he wields.

He wastes no time having the cuffs drag me to the right corner. Sauntering over to stand next to me, Lucifer turns on two spotlights mounted on stands to my right and left.

The light reveals Mistress Codee bound to the wall by demons in shadow form. She keeps her eyes shut against the lights, but overall, she appears serene.

At a gentle wave from Hadeon, the demons shift Lady C. further left, leaving room for the demons guarding Paige to move her into position. They quickly pin her to the right wall, so that she's equidistant between Lady C. and me. Under threat from multiple shadow spikes, Paige submits to a pair of spirit cuffs.

"Show them," Lucifer orders.

The demons release their hold on Lady C. but remain close enough to prevent escape. She already wears spirit cuffs.

Slowly, Lady C.'s body ages backwards until she appears mid-thirties. Her skin tightens and her posture straightens. Gold color sweeps through her hair as it grows past her shoulders. There's a spark of defiance as she looks at Lucifer, but then, her gaze slides left until it fixes upon Paige. Lady C. rests her head back against the wall. Tears stream down her face.

Paige stares intently down at the floor, refusing to give Lucifer the satisfaction of a reaction.

I will help you.

I feel Paige's promise, but I'm careful not to even think a response. Communication, even subtle telepathic communication, is dangerous right now.

Instead, I study Lady C. and Paige. The resemblance between them is unmistakable.

I finally understand the glee in Lucifer's voice.

"I love family reunions," says Lucifer. "Don't you, Hadeon? They're so touching."

Hadeon nods tightly, but his scowl declares displeasure with the scene unfolding.

"It feels like old times," Lucifer comments. "Except instead of dear Josiah, we have Mina as our third guest."

Lady C.'s body flickers as she tries to shift. The spirit cuffs keep forcing her back into human form and the capsule of demons tightens around her. She pulls futilely against the bonds and shakes her head.

"I won't do it," she declares, still shaking her head. "I can't. Not again. You know what happened last time!" Her voice grows stronger with each statement.

"I do indeed," says Lucifer. "Please make every effort to be more delicate this time. I want the Kindred Spirit Bond intact."

A weary, sad expression crosses Lady C.'s features.

"Didn't you learn anything from the last experience?" she wonders. "The bond is a gift from our King. It will never serve you."

I've sent Allister a message, but he's bound with spirit cuffs now controlled by Than.

I don't respond to Paige's report, but I reach out and try to strengthen her spirit.

"Forgive me for not taking your word on the matter, Lady Elizabeth," says Lucifer with mock courtesy. "People don't believe me when I say I'm an optimist, but I believe this matter is important enough to try again. Besides, you're the backup plan." He turns and regards me thoughtfully. "I'm hoping Mina will make this easy on everybody."

"I thought you wanted to take it from me," I say, becoming impatient with Lucifer's games.

"I enjoy the strategy game almost as much as the brute force one," says Lucifer, lifting one shoulder. "Either path to victory will suffice. The only difference is that the harder you make me work, the more everybody suffers."

"Why involve Paige and Mistress Codee?" I ask. "And what does it have to do with Master Josiah? I thought he was your prisoner too."

"He is," says Lucifer. "I'm surprised you haven't made the connections yet, but I suppose you can be excused based on the trials you've endured recently. Perhaps Hadeon will give you a brief history lesson since it was his mission." He sends Hadeon a pointed look.

"Elizabeth and Josiah had a Kindred Spirit Bond," Hadeon explains reluctantly. "I took it from them."

Lucifer holds up a hand to stop him.

"He's being modest," says Lucifer. "He worked very hard to research his foes and learn their weaknesses."

"He kidnapped our infant daughter." Lady C.'s statement sails toward Hadeon with a powerful glare. "When we came for her, he tortured Leora and forced me to break the bond with Josiah."

I consider Paige's given name. It means "compassion" or "light." No wonder Hadeon couldn't drive goodness out of her.

"You remember all that?" Lucifer's voice rises with surprise. "I thought those memories were gone."

"Buried, not gone," Lady C. corrects him. "You saw to that." She moves her desperate gaze to me. "If you don't give him your bond willingly, he wants me to take it." She shuts her eyes tight. "That is why he's threatening her."

"Can you do it?" I wonder.

"I don't know," Lady C. answers softly. Her eyes open, and she lets her gaze slide between Paige and me a few times before settling on me. "The last time I tried, I nearly destroyed Josiah."

"Yes, but you accomplished something nobody has ever done before or since," says Lucifer. He turns to me to see if I'm following his ramblings. "She severed the connection between Josiah's spirit and body."

The reminder makes Lady C. shiver.

"I have no wish to try again," she says, "but I … can't let him hurt her."

Paige's expression flips from stony disbelief to horror to anger. She settles on anger.

"You knew!" she flings the accusation at Hadeon.

"I'm missing something," I murmur.

"I protected you from the knowledge," Hadeon says to Paige, ignoring me. "Would you have refused the order if you knew she was your mother?"

The question diffuses much of Paige's anger, leaving only confusion and despair on her face.

Lucifer yawns and stretches.

"As interesting as these revelations have been, I believe we've reached decision time," he announces. "What will it be, Mina? Will you surrender your Kindred Spirit Bond nicely or will you prolong Lady Elizabeth's torment?"

Neither options sounds good, but he has not stated every possibility.

By design, spirit cuffs limit the will one can exert through their spirit form. Spirit's Bane weakens my mortal body and causes crippling pain whenever I try to use significant spiritual Gifts.

But I am more than these.

"You will not hurt them," I say.

"I take it you're volunteering to go first then." Lucifer gestures subtly.

Paige's demon escort moves her to stand beside her mother while the spirit cuffs deposit me in her place.

The chains linking my wrists together break and stretch my arms wide, holding me fast to the wall.

"This looks familiar," Lucifer comments, drawing out the switchblade. "I think I'll finish what Hadeon started."

I squeeze both hands into fists.

More demon shadows move in and force my hands apart, leaving them wide open for attack.

When Lucifer moves to shove the switchblade through my right hand, I turn it to spirit. The weapon punches a small, neat hole into the wall next to me. I stop the shift midway up my forearm. The transformed part burns from Spirit's Bane.

"Neat trick." Lucifer yanks the blade free and moves it close to my neck. "But it looks painful. Are you sure you want to keep this up?"

Not sparing the energy to reply, I lean back against the wall and close my eyes. I know what I want to do but not exactly how to accomplish it. While I'm thinking, I feel the thin blade slip into my right hand. On the surface, it's a sharp, aching pain but deeper, there's a deadly poison at work. It marches steadily down through my arm, killing the cells as it goes.

Spirit's Bane burns against my chest, eager to destroy the invader.

I stop trying to control its power and completely shift into spirit. The familiar pain magnifies, blasting through the poison.

I can't keep doing this. I'll break.

Show me the way.

The cry gets answered in an unusual manner. I realize Lucifer himself gave me the answer when he recounted Lady C.'s accomplishment. She split spirit and body apart.

What happened to Master Josiah's soul? Did it survive? Where did it go?

There's likely a soul plane of some sort.

As the realization sets in, my vision changes. The wall to my right and everything else turns to cubes and triangles. Each small shape has a number in it. Every number corresponds to shade of gray, silver, or white. The shapes move and shift, creating faces and creatures before dissolving back into the larger landscape again.

"You made it!" The outline of a man forms near Lady C. and Paige. "Hurry, we can still save them, but first, Allister needs us."

Chapter 29:
Collecting Pieces

Case Report #: AK-127
Case Agent: Mistress Adira Clarimond
Guardian: Allister Knight

When two translucent figures suddenly appear behind Abdon, I think I must be hallucinating. It's hard to tell much about them from looks because both appear to be a compilation of tiny random shapes.

The larger one reaches out and pulls Abdon away from me.

The shorter one moves towards me and fades from sight.

Before I can worry about where it went, the spirit cuffs get hot and shake. Sparks fly out from them as they strain to hold me.

I join the effort to break free, pulling with both physical and spiritual strength.

There's a brief burning sensation in my chest as the spirit cuffs shatter.

Next instant, I'm upright and back in spirit. My armor falls into place and Tyre returns.

Let Master Josiah's soul deal with Abdon. We're needed elsewhere.

I turn around, looking for Mina.

An amused sense sweeps over me.

175

I'm here. Go. I'll explain later.

Go where?

Trust Paige.

Those are two words I never thought I'd associate with one another. Maybe Mina had better luck making Paige see sense than I did with Abdon. I glance at Abdon and see he's fully absorbed with his fight against the cube ghost.

Recalling Paige's pictures of the island and the stone ruins, I concentrate on her fourth image, the one with the numbers and symbols. My Earth navigation skills might be rusty, but thankfully, Mina's are not. I access the detailed map of the Earth stored in memory and swiftly zero in on the two locations.

Where to first?

The island.

I should find Roy.

He's with Reena and Aderes.

If I find out you're a demon impersonating Mina, we're going to have serious words later.

Fair enough. Now move.

Taking human form, I teleport to the island coordinates and land knee-deep in muddy water. After wading to shore and climbing out, I switch to clean khaki shorts and a T-shirt since they're more weather appropriate anyway. The shade from several trees offers some relief but the humidity intensifies the oppressive heat, making breathing unpleasant. I almost prefer the dusty gloom of the diamond mine.

We won't be here long.

What are we looking for?

"Who are you?" demands a male voice. "How did you get here?"

Whirling, I face a disheveled man toting a makeshift spear. The ragged remains of cargo shorts are his only clothes. His lean muscles tense.

A warm, rushing sensation hits me the same moment the gray-ghost version of Mina materializes in front of me.

"We've come to take you home, Master Josiah," says Mina.

Once she mentions the name, I recognize him. This version's far thinner than the imposter I exposed, but beneath the ragged beard and deep tan, the features match.

"I am home," declares the man. His voice is raspy with disuse. He clutches the spear tightly, though he doesn't threaten us with it.

"You have another home and people who need you," Mina explains. "I can help you remember, but only if you wish it so."

"I don't believe you," the man says quickly. Fear and suspicion glitter in his dark green eyes.

"But you do believe in things beyond this world," Mina insists. "Your heart is missing something. You've spent years waiting for someone to return."

"You're not her," argues the man.

"No, I am not Elizabeth," Mina agrees, "but if you let me restore you, I can take you to her. She and Leora need you. Even now, they fight a battle begun almost fifteen years ago. We can end it today, but we need you."

Who's Leora?

Paige. Now hush.

"I'm nobody," says the man. "Just a shell of a man and a failure."

"That's a lie put in place by our enemies," says Mina. "You are part of one of the Glorious King's most trusted servants, an angel of light called Josiah. Your name is a reminder of the King's healing power. Let us help you live up to it."

Slowly, the man sinks to the ground and leans heavily upon his spear.

"What must I do?" he wonders. "Why do I feel so incomplete?"

"Your body, soul, and spirit were separated by a terrible accident," Mina explains. "To set things right, we must first collect the pieces. Allister's Teleportation and Transportation Gifts will make that possible. Once he finishes his part, I can restore your mind and soul to your spirit and body, making you whole."

"You're Mina's soul?" I ask tentatively. "How are you able to be here on Earth."

"We can wonder about such things later," she says, nodding to the man. "His family—and my physical form—are

177

still guests of the Prince of Darkness."

"I'm ready," says the man, using his spear to stand. His eyes dart around our surroundings like he suspects demons will jump out of the underbrush. "Let us leave this place."

"You might want to leave the spear behind," I note. "Something tells me, you'll have a much better weapon waiting for you upon restoration."

The man stares at the spear for a lingering moment. Finally, he nods, lifts it up, and drives the end into the dirt.

Mina's soul returns to the place it occupied on our trip to the island.

Touching the man's shoulder, I revert to the last location in the mines.

Not much has changed.

Abdon still trades punches and kicks with the cube ghost version of Master Josiah, which I now recognize as his soul.

Microjumping forward, I take physical form and slam into Abdon. He stumbles back but quickly recovers.

Two more jumps bring me to the body and soul of Master Josiah. They regard each other curiously, but I don't give them time to reminisce. Touching both, I move everybody to the second set of coordinates Paige gave me.

The instant before I teleport, Abdon wraps a despair whip around my ankle. The connection lets him follow, and he knocks into me, sending us both to the floor. I didn't think it'd be possible to find more dust than in the mine, but this abandoned building wins in that regard. I scrape both knees on the rough landing.

The chilly air stabs at me, enhanced by unease at being near so many demons. I can't see them yet, but the dread I'm feeling speaks of a large number.

Master Josiah's body groans as he rolls to a sitting position, stands, and shivers. If I'm feeling the temperature change in my T-shirt and shorts, he must really be uncomfortable without a shirt. His soul hovers near us serenely.

Do not let them know of the soulscape.

Mina is not making much sense, but I gather it means Hadeon and Lucifer are blind to the souls. Abdon's grim expression—and the fact that he's staring straight through Master

Josiah's soul—also confirms this.

Mina's soul returns to her body, which lies near the corner.

Two other prisoners stand chained to the walls near Mina. They're in human form, but I'm guessing they're angels too. Bright light from spotlights obscures their features until my eyes adjust.

I take spirit form. My gold armor brightens the room, causing demons to widen the pocket around us.

In spirit, I instinctively know that the figure to the right is Paige. It takes me a second longer to recognize Lady Elizabeth Codee. She's nothing like the figure I met at Mina's first safehouse. There's a fierceness to her spirit that wasn't there before.

"You're too late, Allister," says Lucifer, "but congratulations on arriving. We were just waiting for Spirit's Bane to finish your friend. It won't be long."

Despite his calm words, there's deep irritation in his eyes.

Particles of dust pass through the light and change course abruptly when they hit a shield. That must be Lady Elizabeth's doing. Paige's focus appears to be on Mina's still form.

"What are you doing here?" Hadeon asks, speaking to Abdon.

"Give me leave to kill him, Master," Abdon says, not taking his eyes off me. He clutches two daggers, one a spirit blade and the other a mortal weapon.

Lucifer waves the words away.

"I'm more interested in why he's keeping company with ragged humans."

"It's Josiah, Master," Hadeon murmurs.

Sadistic joy enters Lucifer.

"That's wonderful news," he says. He microjumps to the space directly in front of Josiah's physical form and conducts a brief visual inspection. He ends with a disapproving noise. "The years have not been kind to you, but no matter. Love is blind." Lucifer claps a hand on Josiah's shoulder. "Come, let us meet the quaint family you abandoned years ago."

I open my mouth to protest, but Mina stops me.

Wait. Lady C.'s shield protects us, but it also keeps you

179

from the final piece.

What final piece?

Master Josiah's spirit.

Where is it?

I have it, but I don't have the strength to get it to you past the shield. You must get Lady C. to lower the shield.

How am I going to do that?

Pray and wait.

It's not a very solid plan, but Lucifer and Mina's temporary goals seem to be aligned.

Cautiously, I move to a better position for observing.

"Do you see who has joined us, Elizabeth?" asks Lucifer. He's brought Master Josiah's mortal form close to the shield. Kicking the man's leg, Lucifer forces him to kneel and conjures a pair of sheers. "Perhaps some grooming will help."

"I don't believe you," Lady Elizabeth says. "You've tried this trick before."

"Come see for yourself," invites Lucifer. "Illusions tend to be a bit more polished." He grips the man's hair and gives it a brief shake, releasing a small cloud of dust. "They smell better too."

Sending the sheers away, he conjures a handgun and presses it to the back of the man's head.

I should so something, right?

Freeze time in both realms. I'm going to try something.

I do as asked, even though I've never considered trying to affect the spirit plane before.

Mina's soul leaves her body again, enters Lady Elizabeth, and pulls her soul to the surface. I can tell because her body looks like it's been fractured into a thousand geometric shapes.

Talk to her.

"Mistress Codee, we need you to lower the shield," I say.

There's no verbal response, but her entire body shakes violently.

"Please, I know it sounds crazy, but we can restore him," I promise.

A resounding *no* explodes in my head, breaking my tenuous grasp on time.

Lucifer glances at me suspiciously before returning to his

bad guy speech.

"Last chance. Obey or watch this part of him die."

Chapter 30:
Do You Trust Me?

Case Report #: MN-128
Case Agents: Master Blaz and Mistress Codee
Guardian: Mina Nadir

My time in Seriana—that's what Master Josiah called the soulscape—was brief but informative. I learned two important things. One, how to defeat Spirit's Bane, and two, how to find and help Allister. Following a hastily laid plan, I successfully brought Allister and Master Josiah's body into the heart of the conflict.

I did not anticipate Lady C.'s strong reaction. I don't need to think forward the possible futures to know I have to change it. The most obvious one consumes my thoughts. If we can't convince Lady C. to trust us, Master Josiah's physical form will die. Then, his soul and spirit will remain stuck in their respective realms. Between the poisoned blade and Spirit's Bane, my body is almost gone as well. Lady C. and Paige can probably hold out for several days, but eventually, the demons will overwhelm them. Only Allister stands a moderate chance of escaping.

I can only heal my body if my spirit is free to work. That means I need to deal with Spirit's Bane, but I can't do that until I have proper help. The most capable help is currently scattered across three planes or near at hand but utterly broken.

I can't save us and neither can Allister.

It's the most humbling, terrifying thought I could have.

Lucifer's finger already rests on the handgun's trigger.

Enough time exists for one quick message.

One more move.

Allister, do you trust me?

I barely get his affirmative answer before making my move. Yanking his soul clear out of his body, I merge him with Master Josiah's physical form. At the same time, I move my soul close to Lady C. and place a hand on her shoulder. She might not feel the direct contact in her physical form, but the sentiment should still reach her. The Kindred Spirit Bond that once connected them does so again through us.

Lucifer fires.

Lady C. recognizes Josiah and drops the shield.

Josiah microjumps diagonally two feet forward and one foot right.

Lady C. puts the shield back in place.

The bullet slams into the ground and ricochets up toward Lady C.'s stomach. Suddenly, it freezes as Master Josiah uses Allister's Gift to shut down time in the mortal realm.

Hadeon and Lucifer direct every demon present to wear down the shield.

I ignore their frantic orders and threats, relegating them to background noise.

The shield will collapse soon, but we've bought a few minutes.

Lady C. and Master Josiah lock eyes.

I wish I could give them time to reunite properly, but I need Josiah to bring in Allister before Lucifer and Hadeon think to threaten him. Also, I'm not sure how long my friend's spirit and body can function without his soul. Master Josiah aside, the three cords were never meant to be separated.

It takes some careful coordination, but Master Josiah manages to bring Allister into the fold.

Nine demons slip through too.

Decked out in full spirit armor, Allister calls Tyre and tears through the demons. His fighting style without his soul lacks much in the way of grace, but the confined space within the shielded area gives the demons little room to retreat.

After the fight, Allister blinks and looks around at us, confused.

Free Paige.

Master Josiah too stares down at his hands in wonder. His gaze goes from there to the bullet to Lady C. to Paige. Through the connection, I feel his heartbeats quicken. Her eyes are closed in concentration, so she doesn't sense his attention. For the last several minutes, Paige has been pouring strength into me. It's likely the only reason my body has survived this long.

"How?" Master Josiah's shoulders slump and his head dips.

Together.

Carefully, I extricate Allister's soul and return it to his body. Next, I explain my plan to Lady C., Master Josiah, and Allister.

My friend drops to his knees beside my body. It's strange to see his anguish through another's eyes.

You can't help me yet. Paige must be next.

That much I'm certain about. Between the two of them, Allister and Master Josiah might have enough strength of will and experience to break a single set of spirit cuffs. Dealing with Spirit's Bane will require Master Josiah, Allister, Lady C., and I to be at full strength. As Paige's parents, the others won't be able to devote their full attention to anything while she remains in danger. Once free of the spirit cuffs, Paige's strength should return to normal. She can then help free her mother. Finally, Paige does not possess healing gifts, but Lady C.'s very minor Gift can be enhanced through Allister's Transfer abilities. In theory, that should allow her to heal me enough to completely restore Master Josiah.

I don't need to explain my reasoning. The Kindred Spirit Bond conveys my feelings accurately. The others—especially Allister—don't necessarily agree with my logic, but they do trust me.

Please, hurry. The bullet won't remain suspended forever.

Even with Master Josiah's skillful manipulation, time will eventually right itself and speed forward fractionally to recover the lost moments. Lady C. needs to be moved before then.

Allister and Master Josiah dutifully go to Paige and each

184

grip one of the spirit cuffs. They struggle because each is missing a vital part of themselves. Of the two, only Allister has a spirit so this task rests largely with him. I can direct and encourage, but my own spirit lies locked away within my dying body.

Almost a minute passes before I remember I don't need my spirit to help. I have something better. Using the Kindred Spirit Bond, I link my soul to Lady C.'s, then to Allister, and finally to Master Josiah. Once I weave through these connections several times, I bid them to try again.

Part of Allister's spirit moves to Master Josiah for a split-second.

It's enough.

The spirit cuffs shatter.

Paige launches into Master Josiah's arms.

A sense of peace radiates from them, but the work's not done yet.

We need to stop that bullet.

My announcement breaks up the happy reunion. I run through some quick calculations. We have less than a minute before time proceeds. Given the time it took to break Paige free. We'll never make it.

Prop my body up in front of Lady Elizabeth.

The idea meets fierce resistance.

"Your body won't survive a bullet," Allister says.

My body is unconscious. I probably won't feel it.

While we argue, Paige pulls free of her father and stands in front of her mother.

"Let it happen," she says.

"No!" The cry comes from Lady C. and Master Josiah.

Allister and I echo it silently.

Lady C. strains against the spirit cuffs but they hold.

"Please, not again," Lady C. begs. "We lost you for fifteen years! I can't do that again."

"I don't have healing gifts," Paige argues. "You do."

With the knowledge granted by the Kindred Spirit Bond, I realize Paige speaks truth. What I have been calling Lady C.'s *minor healing Gift* is only a faint echo of what it was at the height of her power.

She's right. You're the only one with the natural gifting

for a healing of this sort, but you need to help us with the spirit cuffs first. You can't do that with a bullet wound.

"Let me do it," says Master Josiah. "It was meant for me anyway."

I gently let him know that similar reasoning applies.

Even without a third of your being, you are the strongest among those who remain free. And I don't know if a wound will interfere with what I need to do to fix the fractures that keep your body, spirit, and soul apart.

"What about me?" asks Allister. "I'm whole and I have healing abilities through you."

You also have the most experience breaking spirit cuffs.

Paige smiles tightly and glares at the still bullet.

"Never thought it would come to this," she muses.

Frustrated tears flow down Lady C.'s face.

When you're free, we will right this.

I direct the promise to Lady C. alone.

"I'm ready," Paige says, letting her eyes shut.

Wait. Move an inch to your right, kneel, and lean forward slightly.

I check her position and the bullet's trajectory to calculate a path with the most stopping power that won't immediately kill her.

Catching on, Allister does the same calculations. Coming to the same conclusion, he gently positions Paige before nodding to Master Josiah who lets time move forward.

The bullet slams into Paige's left shoulder.

Allister catches her and helps her to the ground, positioning her right hand over the wound.

With Paige's blood still on his hands, Allister grabs hold of Lady C.'s left wrist and waits for Master Josiah to move into position at her right wrist. As before, they work in concert, using Allister's spirit to weaken the spiritual bindings.

When they finally succeed, Lady C. drops besides Paige and cries.

Something's wrong. She's still bound.

The spirit cuffs are gone, but the years of guilt still have a strong grip on her.

Master Josiah, your daughter needs us. There's a

brokenness in Lady C. that Allister and I cannot reach, but I believe you can.

"What's wrong with her?" Master Josiah wonders.

She fears to lose you both again.

Master Josiah goes to Lady C. and hugs her, whispering reassurances.

Allister and I retreat to my body to give them some privacy, but there's nowhere to go that's far enough to not hear everything that's said.

We have another problem.

This thought gets planted directly into Allister's head. He raises an eyebrow in question.

If she doesn't recover quickly, the shield will fail.

As we watch, cracks appear in the bubble surrounding us. As the cracks widen, a demon slips inside and dives for Paige.

Ironically, that's exactly what we need.

Lady C. screams, turns her hands to spirit, and shoves them through the demon. The contact between their spirits sends the demon reeling.

The shield renews, stronger than before.

There's still fear within Lady C., but it's drowned out by love and a mother's protective instinct.

The blood loss has put Paige into a listless state.

Lady C. places both hands over the wound.

I feel her straining to reach her healing Gift.

Nothing happens.

We're wrong again. I'm wrong again.

"About what?" Allister asks.

What's the most basic thing we've learned about the Kindred Spirit Bond?

"We can use each other's Gifts," Allister answers.

We lock eyes before turning to take in Lady C.'s new battle.

Exactly.

Allister's knees crack as he rises. Settling down between Lady C. and Paige, he places one hand on Paige's sweaty forehead and the other on Lady C.'s right shoulder.

Master Josiah moves to Paige's other side and places his left hand on his daughter's good shoulder and his right hand on

Lady C.'s head.

Power flows through our small circle. I direct the work. Lady C. performs the bulk of the healing. Allister and Master Josiah lend strength and support to both Lady C. and the patient, making sure both have exactly what they need to succeed.

Chapter 31:
Philosophical Discussion

Case Report #: AK-128
Case Agent: Mistress Adira Clarimond
Guardian: Allister Knight
Once the bullet is removed from Paige's shoulder, Lady Codee knits together the flesh and repairs the internal damage. Paige's human form will need rest to fully heal from the trauma, but her spirit's still strong and spoiling for a fight. Lady Codee and Master Josiah want her to let them handle the massive battle waiting to happen on the other side of the lady's shield. Mina and I kind of want to keep out of the family disagreement, but we're literally connected to it.

With time running out, we host an argument.

"Help me ... turn to ... spirit," says Paige. Pain and tension keep her shoulders stiff.

Having long shared Mina's ability to quickly switch forms, I take for granted that transitions are much slower for most other beings. It became so effortless that I forgot it takes some physical strength to accomplish.

"If you stay in human form, the demons won't be able to touch you," Master Josiah argues.

"Once I drop the full shield, I can maintain one around you," says Lady Codee.

"I can ... fight." Paige glares up at her parents.

189

In spirit, she should have access to most of her Gifts.

It can be hard to tell tone with thoughts, but Mina sounds neutral on the issue.

"Need to … help." The plea in Paige's eyes seems genuine.

"Being in spirit will let her body rest," I add, throwing my support to Paige.

Master Josiah fingers his long, ragged beard. He's still sporting the island refugee look, but the wisdom in his eyes is unmistakable.

"Without strength from your physical form, your spirit may falter," Master Josiah points out. "You'll be vulnerable to reset or worse."

Once upon a time, I'd wonder about his *worse* comment, but given that he's still minus his spirit, there's no need to dig for elaboration.

Many of the demons out there were recently your allies. Do you still wish to fight them?

Mina's question pains Paige, but it's one that needs an answer. I think we can trust her but gauging her emotions through Mina's Empathy Gift isn't the same as knowing them through a Kindred Spirit Bond.

"Can they … be saved?"

Paige's question causes a moment of silence.

"I don't know," I admit. "Most seem committed."

My gaze wanders up to the shield which flashes yellow and red where demons repeatedly throw their essences into breaking it down.

I might be able to help with that.

Mina quickly explains that the view through the soulscape can help distinguish between dark souls that serve Lucifer whole-heartedly and those that haven't truly embraced that path. There are no guarantees, but the latter type may be redeemable. Everybody gets a crash course in seeing the world through the soulscape.

The world turns into small shapes. Finding the view disorienting, I turn the ability off almost immediately, but I let it linger in me so it transfers to Paige. The tension in her shoulders relaxes.

"Please … I need this," Paige pleas.

Master Josiah and Lady Codee exchange a long, worried look before nodding consent.

Mina takes the lead in easing Paige's transformation to spirit form.

Black leather armor appears on her as Paige rises and summons a long, thin sword.

"That's new," I comment, taking in her battle mode.

Tiny metal pieces embedded in the leather make it shiny. A piece of each bracer extends over Paige's hands. A line of throwing daggers encircles her waist. Tall black boots and kneecap armor protect her legs. The outfit initially features a black cloth mask across the lower half of her face, but Paige immediately pulls it down so it settles at her neck. Her blond hair is now caught up in a pair of braids pinned to her head.

"Special occasion," she says, stepping back toward the wall.

We have one more battle before the demons arrive.

Guilt kicks me for forgetting Mina.

It's time to deal with Spirit's Bane.

I expect such an announcement to be followed by detailed instructions on position and energy flow to prepare for an epic spiritual battle. Instead, my friend merely asks one question.

Master Josiah, are you ready?

Bowing his head and shutting his eyes, Master Josiah nods. Tears run down his cheeks and onto his beard. He drops to his knees.

The gold stream of particles I've come to recognize as Mina in her soul form stretches between her still body and Master Josiah. He sways and starts to fall.

I catch his shoulders and ease him down into the space Paige just vacated.

More cracks appear in the shield.

Three demons slip inside.

"I'm losing the shield," Lady Codee says grimly.

"Shrink it around them," I order, getting a better grip on Master Josiah.

Careful not to disrupt the connection, I drag Master Josiah over to Mina's body and lay him down next to her.

191

When they're settled, I glance at Paige.

"I'm ready," she says.

"Do you want to stay here in the corner or have more room to maneuver?" I ask.

"We should both keep to the corner. It's more defensible," Paige answers before firing a question. "Do you want high or low?"

"Low." I smile as I say it. Excitement and anticipation swell inside me.

"Be careful," Lady Codee warns. "You'll have to fight together, especially if Lucifer or Hadeon join the fight."

Before we can strategize, Lady Codee's shield collapses. In its place, she erects two more. One shimmers to life around Mina and Master Josiah, and the other forms around herself.

Paige and I immediately engage the demons.

Having fought Paige several times, I know enough to stay out of her way. Thankfully, she's taken responsibility for the ceiling battle, so our chances of accidentally stabbing each other are low.

I don't exactly have time to admire her ruthless efficiency at dispatching demons, but the panicked pitch and frequency of shrieks from above tell me she's doing fine. I'm also getting showered in nasty demon dust.

Four demons dart at me from different angles. I release Tyre to guard my back and summon Mina's spirit sword, Kentaro, to deal with the two I'm facing. They try to dodge, but a downward slash catches both and turns them to dust.

Almost a minute passes in a blur of violent encounters with demons before I realize I'm subtly being herded away from Mina and Master Josiah. I slide backwards to recover the lost ground while keeping up the fight. Tyre and Kentaro are both in hand, but I release Mina's sword to establish a two-handed grip on my spirit sword. Kentaro zooms toward Mina and halts abruptly.

With a sinking feeling, I spirit flash and run straight into an invisible wall. A distinct sense of Abdon hits me as I bounce off the shield and fall into a defensive stance. He's crouching near one of the two spotlights shining on the corner where the battle began.

Testing a theory, I jab Tyre into the space in front of me. It's like striking a metal plate, but I have the satisfaction of seeing Abdon flinch. Grimly, I recall Mina's lesson on seeing through the soulscape. Soon, the colors and shapes of the world shift. Where once I saw nothing, I now see translucent red walls criss-crossing the room.

Turning off the special view, I check in on the others.

Paige still battles demons across the ceiling. More dive at Lady Codee who concentrates on maintaining the protective case around Mina and Master Josiah. Nothing seems to have changed with them.

Lucifer's unaccounted for.

That's worrisome.

Hadeon's to my left with his hands outstretched. Most of the red lines connect to him, telling me he's responsible for the bulk of them.

I try to microjump to him and run into a wall again. At least I can see it this time.

A wall behind me disappears to allow a new batch of demons to enter. It's back in place before I can microjump or spirit flash through. Annoyed with the trick, I tear through the demons. Every time I get close to one wall, one opens from the opposite side, letting in yet more demons. Abdon must be using his shield walls to sense me. Catching on, I finally get smart and fill Tyre with a section of my spirit and send him to the far wall. Then, I wait. As expected, the shield before me drops to grant entry to more demons. I microjump through and recall Tyre. He slips through just before Abdon's shield reforms.

I tense as several emotions charge through me. Anger and helplessness top the list.

I've found Lucifer.

He's inside the corner section with Mina, Lady Codee, and Master Josiah. More specifically, he's looming over my friend while a solid-looking black wall of interlocked demons traps Master Josiah and Lady Codee on the left half of the makeshift prison.

Slamming Tyre repeatedly against the shield does nothing.

Laying hands on the shield and intensifying my spirit

presence makes Abdon wince and sends a burning sensation up my arms.

Screaming my frustration, I assume human form and ram the shield. I bounce off hard and fall. Back in spirit, I scramble to think of a way in.

Lucifer turns toward me slowly and smiles. A lazy gesture from him causes the shield in front of me to change enough to let sound pass easier.

"Allister, nice of you to take time away from beating my servants," says Lucifer. "Perhaps you'll have better luck getting Paige to see reason."

"Why would I do that?" I demand. My mind clouds with righteous anger as my eyes stab into the Prince of Darkness.

Lucifer turns sideways so I get a clearer view of my friend.

"I was about to indulge in a philosophical discussion with dear Mina," he says, crossing his arms over his chest. "It will be a much more pleasant experience for her if you cooperate."

Mina hasn't moved, but subtle movement shows me she's still breathing.

Paige!

I heard him.

Squinting into the gloom, I can see Paige standing almost directly opposite of me. She's stopped shredding demons, but still clutches her spirit sword. Looking up, she addresses the demons, but I cannot hear her words.

By the time I return my attention to Lucifer, he's propped Mina against the right wall.

Her head flops to the left.

"If you'd like to beg me to have mercy, I'm listening." Lucifer watches me carefully.

Swallowing the urge to follow the suggestion, I silently pray for wisdom, strength, and patience.

"Nothing to say from either of you? That's surprising." Lucifer swivels his head to address the comments to both Paige and me. "Let's begin."

Two mild shocks lift Mina to consciousness.

Lucifer kneels in front of her and picks up her left hand, squeezing gently. He waits patiently until she opens her eyes and lifts her head before beginning his interrogation.

"What did you do with Spirit's Bane?" He fingers the pendant still attached to a thin chain around Mina's neck.

The center diamond is gone.

"I released him," Mina replies. "It was mostly Master Josiah's trapped spirit."

Lucifer shifts his grip on her left hand.

I don't see what happens, but Mina shudders.

I slam my fist against the shield. It flickers but holds.

"You're lying," Lucifer states.

Mina shakes her head.

"Somebody probably lied to you, but it wasn't me," she says.

"Why would Josiah attack you?" Lucifer asks.

"I don't think he meant to," answers Mina. "I think the pain was a cry for help. One I didn't understand for a long time."

Judging by Lucifer's expression, he doesn't like her answer. He lets go of the pendant and moves his right hand over the one he holds.

Mina flinches again.

"Stop it!" I don't care if I sound desperate. I need to break through this shield.

"Where is your beloved King now?" Lucifer hisses the question.

"Always with me," Mina replies.

Standing, Lucifer looks down at Mina.

"You are alone," he points out softly. "Your King has abandoned you. Perhaps he hates you."

"Never." Mina's protest sounds weaker than I'd like.

"You don't even have the strength to transform to spirit, do you?" Lucifer's question holds contempt. He conjures a dagger and throws it at Mina's right arm. It opens a shallow cut along her forearm before clattering to the ground. "Pick it up and fight back!"

I can't watch anymore. Sending Kentaro and Tyre away, I bring them back out of the Veil beyond the shield and send them toward Abdon. He knocks them aside easily, but it's enough to break his concentration.

Gathering my spiritual strength, I burst through and ram

into Lucifer. I'm tempted to continue the fight, but instead, I stand guard over Mina.

He staggers left and instinctively dons spirit armor. The black plates form around him. A shiny silver sword appears in his right hand.

"I will—"

Before Lucifer can even utter his threat, Master Josiah and Lady Codee beat Hadeon's shield much the same as I did.

Together, they send out strong beams of pure light that leave my eyes dazzled. Master Josiah holds a brilliant longsword in his right hand.

The demons flee to the ceilings, regroup, and attack.

Lady Codee throws several beams of light directly into Lucifer's chest, knocking him further left long enough for her to create a new shield for Mina.

I microjump to Master Josiah's side and join the battle.

With wild battle cries, the demons attack together.

Master Josiah's longsword, Darius, snaps out like a striking snake, crashing into eight demons before I have time to sweep Tyre through the three in front of me. The moves carry us apart from each other. I want to rejoin him. At first, I'm afraid I'll get in the way, but then, an odd feeling of peace descends upon my spirit. The feeling also carries a sense of familiarity, and I remember Jabir sharing his skills and memories with me.

A new section of demons flow toward Master Josiah's back. I spirit flash through them, dragging Tyre through the lot of them. From then on, we fight with a fluid grace only born of countless hours of practice together. I'm not sure whether to attribute the connection to the Kindred Spirit Bond or Jabir's work, but I'm grateful for it.

While Master Josiah and I battle most of the demons, Paige hovers near Lady Codee who is still protecting Mina.

At last, the demons retreat to the ceiling. Lucifer impatiently brushes some dust off his suit.

Hadeon and Abdon cringe at the amount of demon dust covering the ruins. They hadn't entered the sword contest with us because they'd been busy directing the demon hordes. Both look ready to continue the fight.

Only Lucifer seems aloof. He looks around at each of us

with obvious disdain. Every hair on his head is in place since he spent the battle behind a strong personal shield.

I don't have time to wonder why he didn't join the fight himself.

"We've accomplished what we came for," says Lucifer. He gestures to Mina's still form. "She'll be dead soon. Mourn her. Then, prepare yourselves. I will avenge every servant slain today." His gaze lingers on Paige. "And punish every traitor."
As soon as Lucifer disappears, the cloud of demons rises and dissipates.

Chapter 32:
Preparing for Future Conflict

Dear Than,

I am not pleased that the boy escaped you, but you acquitted yourself well in the battle that followed. Thank you for helping with the shielding endeavor. I find no flaw with your technique, though your speed could be improved. Strategy as well. Keep practicing. Shielding might come across as a useless skill, but when done well, it can give us a powerful edge in any prolonged fight.

When we encounter the Kindred Spirit Pair again, we will have to work together to divide and conquer. Future conflict is inevitable. They are dangerous enemies. We came close to victory, but despite the battle ending in a draw, we took heavy losses. That said, do not be disturbed by the spirits who shirked their duties. Rest in this simple fact: if they could be swayed by a few fancy words, they never truly served our Dark Master. We are better off without their disloyal service.

Vengeance should not be your primary objective. However, if you come across any traitors on future missions, I trust you know how to treat them.

The loss of Daeva pains me more than the others. Her skills make her worth several legions of normal servants. I take her defection as a personal affront because I invested much in her training. I'm considering you for the team entrusted with our revenge. What are your thoughts on the matter?

Daeva's treachery will not go unpunished, but I cannot help but think her defection rather convenient for you. If I find you had a hand in it beyond that clumsy message to the Dark Master about her deviations from proper protocol, you will experience the full measure of my displeasure. Also, if you ever go above my head on any matter in the future, great or small, I will make you regret it.

I know you believe you deserve to step into Daeva's position, but you still need a mentor. I saw the longing in your spirit when you observed the Kindred Spirit Pair. It's a natural feeling, but you must learn to purge such sentimental emotions from your system when the job demands it. I had hoped Paige would unofficially fulfill the mentor role and save me the trouble of formalizing the assignment.

Deimos will be assuming that position for the foreseeable future. This is not a sign of distrust, only the way of things. You should be honored Deimos has agreed to be your mentor. He has not taken an apprentice in several centuries.

Deimos sees potential in you. Do not waste his time with overly complicated schemes. Trust his teachings. Learn everything you can. If you follow these pieces of advice, it will go well with you.

By the way, the Dark Master suggested I turn the remnants of Daeva's forces over to you as a reward for your excellent service yesterday. I will consider it if you pass your probation period and if your mentor agrees you deserve it.

Good luck with your training. I look forward to hearing of the glory you earn.

Hadeon, Servant of the Dark Master,
Director of Operations

***

Dear Master,

I won't pretend to hide my disappointment with the events that unfolded yesterday, but I trust in your wisdom.

When did you first sense light in Daeva? She served me well for many years. Her turn seemed abrupt because I could not sense her feelings. Forgive me for the lapse. I will consult those who have such gifts more often and test the loyalty of my servants regularly.

Speaking of testing, Deimos measured the loyalty of each demon Daeva commanded. Most met his approval, and the few who failed have already been dealt with. Those who passed will be temporarily assigned to other legions until Than can prove himself worthy of them.

Deimos checked on the prisoner and confirmed your prediction. The spirit we thought of as Josiah was indeed a shadow spirit. Those guarding him testify that he disappeared. Though none can attest to the timing, I believe it lines up with the girl's work during the battle.

What exactly did she do, Master?

I gather she fused Josiah's body, spirit, and soul together, but how did she even find his soul? Are the rumors true? Is there a soul plane? More importantly, if it exists, does this soul plane pose a threat to us? I shall put some theorists to the task of considering such matters, but your insights are always welcome.

Meanwhile, there is still hope for the Spirit's Bane project.

I personally dealt with the fool who lied about its origin. His interrogation was lengthy but enlightening. Turns out he was extraordinarily lucky. His jewelry shop happened to be near our confrontation with Josiah and Elizabeth. When the bond broke and fractured Josiah, his spirit ended up inside one of the cutting diamonds. The jeweler recognized something significant had happened but could not predict what, so he hid the diamond and experimented with it in secret. Over time, those experiments got bolder.

Demons in the area felt its power and reported it to me. The dark angels I sent to investigate discovered that traveling in spirit with the artifact proved painful. When confronted, the man claimed to have been working on creating a weapon to affect spirits. He had ties to a minor cult, so his claim seemed legitimate. It's long been my desire to create such a thing. That wish has seeped out into the world as legend.

The working theory is that Josiah's spirit clung to the diamond and tried to communicate with anything it sensed. Being a spirit, he could only affect other spirits, but without his soul or much of his mind, the best he could accomplish was causing pain.

I'm not sure how the girl solved that mystery. When I find her, I will ask. We must capture the Kindred Spirit Pair again, especially the girl. She is the key to creating more Spirit's Bane artifacts.

I know you think this project borders on obsession but think of the benefits. If we succeed, the entire war will change. No more games. No more resets. We could destroy the armies of light for good.

I have been approaching this wrong. We do not need to steal the bond, only repurpose it.

Creating Spirit's Bane involves more than separating spirit from body and stuffing it into a piece of metal or a precious stone, though that is part of the process. We need the power of the bond and someone who can control it. Mina has proven that she can do both. I will have to work on motivating her. Perhaps she'll respond well to the idea of peace. This war has taken its toll on both sides. Ending it must have some innate appeal.

We would also have to destroy the minds of the spirits being harvested. In a way, the mind unites body, spirit, and soul. My servants could accomplish that in more traditional manners, but I suspect the kind of damage we seek is best inflicted by the Kindred Spirit Bond. Its power lies in the ability to bind spirits and souls together. Therefore, it follows that it also has the capacity to destroy spirits and souls more thoroughly than conventional means.

For now, I will task my servants with tracking our enemies. When the time comes to collect candidates, we will be ready.

Your humble servant,
Hadeon

Part 5:
Peace

Chapter 33:
Changing Everything

Case Report #: MN-129
Case Agents: Master Blaz and Mistress Codee
Guardian: Mina Nadir

After Lucifer, Hadeon, Abdon, and most of the demons flee, we pause and enjoy the peaceful moment. Much work remains, but we need to regroup. I'm not exactly in peak condition anyway.

Paige and Master Josiah watch anxiously.

Allister drops to his knees beside me and tentatively touches my left hand. Healing power flows from him in halting streams like he's afraid to hurt me. Lady Codee places a hand on Allister's head. Her power combines with his and moves through me in steadier waves.

It takes me a few seconds to relax my body enough to accept the healing and join the effort. Carefully, we mend the fingers Lucifer broke, deal with the remaining poison, create new cells to replace the dead ones, and erase the damage inflicted by Spirit's Bane. Slowly, my body adjusts to working with my spirit again, something I've not experienced for months.

When the healing completes, I drop into twilight state, then ease into spirit, flip to soul form, and finally return to my human body.

Allister takes his human form, leaps to his feet, pulls me up, and holds me tight.

The others withdraw a few steps to give us the illusion of

privacy.

I don't need the Kindred Spirit Bond to know Allister worried about me. Each rapid heartbeat thudding against my ear declares it. Returning his hug fiercely, I shut my eyes and let the storm of his emotions play their course. Relief and joy dominate, but there's also fear and suppressed anger. A similar mixture of feelings swirls in my chest too, but Empathy affords me enough emotional space to let them flow instead of building up.

My eyes open again when Allister loosens his grip and holds me at arm's length.

Our eyes meet and lock.

Allister tries to smile. On the third attempt, he partially succeeds. Letting out a big breath, he pulls me forward and rests his forehead against mine. His arms embrace me again, gently this time.

"I missed you," he says.

Tipping my head up, I plant a soft kiss on his lips, knowing it will change everything.

"Likewise," I whisper. My stomach flutters.

Allister jerks his head back in surprise. Confusion and cautious hope flicker across his features.

"Did you—do you … mean that?" Allister asks.

I give him an impatient look and suppress a sarcastic thought about kissing the first thing with a pulse.

"Of course, I mean it," I answer. "I'm sorry I've placed our friendship on the line, but if my time in exile taught me anything, it's that we might not have—"

I don't even get to finish my speech.

A sense of wonder and joy bursts out of Allister and surrounds me. His kiss is long and heartfelt.

"You know this is permanent, right?" he whispers, when the kiss concludes.

"I should hope so," I reply.

Allister steps back slightly but hangs on to my hands.

"We'll need to seek the king's approval," he says. Seriousness sweeps over him. "And the Council. And our masters. And—"

Master Josiah clears his throat.

"Many details will need to be addressed later, but there

are other matters that must be considered before that."

I peer over Allister's shoulder to observe the others.

Lady Codee and Master Josiah stand between us and Paige. Their body language clearly states that their protective instincts have kicked in very strongly. Lady Codee's appearance hasn't changed much since the shift Lucifer forced, but almost everything about Master Josiah has been altered. Instead of the long, unkempt beard, he sports a neatly trimmed goatee. It gives him a distinguished look. The ragged cargo shorts have been replaced with nicer tan dress slacks. He also wears a white button-down shirt and stands taller, seeming to have fully recovered from the years of hard living. He's come a long way from the deserted island in the Pacific Ocean.

"This isn't necessary," says Paige. "I will go with them if they ask it." Her voice carries heavy regret and a newfound humility.

"No!" Lady Codee doesn't speak loudly, but she looks determined to back up the word with force. "We can't trust the Council."

"We'll talk later," I whisper to Allister, squeezing his hands once before letting go. I step around him so that we're side-by-side.

"We'll go directly to the King and beg him for mercy," says Master Josiah.

He and Lady Codee look frightened by the possibility of rejection and the uncertainty of Paige's future.

My heart aches to comfort them.

"We'd never reach the King without the Council's approval," Paige notes. "And I doubt we'll get close to the Council without guidance from Allister and Mina."

"We don't have to go through the Council," says Master Josiah, keeping his eyes on Allister and me. "We'll go someplace safe and seek the King through prayer. He'll find us."

"No place on Earth is safe," Allister argues. "The demons might have fled this time, but they'll be back in much greater numbers. Come to the Heavens with us."

"Our chances of hiding them on Earth are slim," I conclude, drawing everybody's attention, "but the physical universe isn't our only option."

"What did you have in mind?" Master Josiah's tone tells me he suspects my answer.

"Seriana," I answer.

Master Josiah winces but nods and explains for the others.

"If we stay in soul form, we should be able to hide within the soulscape." He hesitates, looking sadly at Paige and Lady Codee. "It's vast and dangerous, but I am familiar with it. The hardest part would be returning."

Lady Codee focuses on me.

"How do you intend to find us once we leave?" she wonders.

"We are connected," I reply. To prove my point, I reach out with my spirit and brush hers. "You should always be able to find us, and likewise, we should always be able to reach you."

"We'll go to the Council and seek an audience with the King," Allister adds.

"Once everything is set, we'll open the way for you to return," I promise. Allister gives me a strange look, so I explain. "In many cases, the soulscape can only be accessed from the outside."

"We'd be trapped until you release us," Paige says.

"Hey, don't you trust us?" asks Allister, picking up on Paige's grim tone.

She holds up a hand to placate him.

"I trust your intentions and your conviction, but not your optimism," Paige clarifies. "A hundred things could go wrong and prevent you from fulfilling your word."

I nod agreement.

"If that is the case, then you'll have to rely upon Master Josiah's original plan," I say. "Prayer. The King can find you anywhere."

"Why didn't he release Josiah all those years?" asks Lady Codee.

"You'll have to ask him for sure, but I suspect the answer stands behind you," I say, waving toward Paige.

"You think he let them suffer because of me?" Paige's question is soft and vulnerable.

Gently pushing past Master Josiah and Lady Codee, I hug Paige even though it's like embracing a block of wood.

"I'm explaining this poorly," I say. "I cannot answer for the King, but I do know his heart and that he loves you very deeply." I tighten my grip as I sense her resistance melting. "In light of that knowledge, I don't think he'd say any price was too high to bring you out of darkness." Finally releasing Paige, I utter one more promise. "I must go soon, but I will be there when you meet the King."

"We both will," Allister says.

To give Paige time to compose herself, Master Josiah and I take turns explaining what we know of Seriana. Peering across the soulscape and entering it are vastly different. It's like the spirit plane but more difficult to enter and exit. Unlike the spiritual and physical realms, one cannot hide their allegiance when viewed through Seriana. That's how I finally saw Paige's spark of light.

After our brief explanations, Master Josiah and I help Paige and Lady Codee take soul form and slip into the soulscape.

"Thank you," says Master Josiah. "I never would have found them without you." He looks like he wishes to say more, but instead, he bows his head and joins the others in Seriana.

Once alone, I reach out for Allister. He takes my hand tentatively, a deep frown fixed in place.

"Don't think about it," I say.

"Think about what?" he asks.

"Any of the bad parts," I answer. Accessing Allister's Transportation Gift, I move us into the Heavens together. "We're both whole and out of Lucifer's reach."

"He'll keep coming," Allister laments.

"One problem at a time," I remind him. Reluctantly, I release my friend's hand. "Let's see the state of the Council and ask for an audience with the King."

I look around and realize that I've brought us to the courtyard in front of the Council's official meeting chamber.

"Do you suspect trouble?" asks Allister, picking up on my serious tone.

"I see the world differently now," I say, peering at the two guards flanking the large doors.

Thankfully, they appear devoted to the task entrusted to them.

"You can turn off the view through the soulscape," Allister points out.

"Yes, I often do that, but I don't want to forget the skill." I struggle to articulate my second fear. A feeling of dread slips over me.

Allister studies me a moment before nodding slowly.

"You're afraid of what we'll find," he comments.

"We found evidence of light and good in demons and dark angels," I say quietly. "It follows that we may also find the opposite."

We fall silent to absorb the horror of that idea.

"We can't control the choices of others, but we'll face them together," Allister promises. "Besides, seeds of doubt don't necessarily doom anybody."

I cling to the hope in his last statement as we approach the guards.

Chapter 34:
Before the Council

Case Report #: AK-129
Case Agent: Mistress Adira Clarimond
Guardian: Allister Knight

Assembling the Council of Light doesn't take long. Lady A. must have had everybody on standby waiting for us. Not sure how she accomplished that given the situation as I left it, but things seem to have settled. I'm relieved to see her take one of the raised seats arrayed before us. This chamber is less formal than the last one I encountered the Council in, but I'm still not eager to face them again. Mina wasn't present when they put me on trial for Transfer, but she can follow my feelings as if they belong to her.

Master Blaz calls the session to order and bids Mina to give her report first. She recounts everything from her first posting as a guardian up until being captured by Paige and taken to the abandoned church in Craco, Italy. I knew most of it, but not the parts about the chase across New Jersey, New York, and Pennsylvania or healing Paige before Roy and I arrived in Texas. The thought of Roy sends guilt through me. I should ask about him.

"Do you have anything to add, Allister?" inquires Master Blaz.

Quickly, I tell my side of the story starting from leaving Lady A.'s office in a hurry up through the battle. Assuming Mina has a good reason to skim over some big story sections concerning the meeting with Satan and company, I do the same. I thought the first point might be awkward because I'd left Lady A. in a precarious situation. She seems none the worse for it, but I still feel like I missed something huge.

"You haven't missed much," Lady A. assures me with a knowing grin. "We've mostly been arguing in circles, as usual. With Lucifer otherwise occupied, there haven't been many crises to attend to."

"How can you make light of this, Adira?" demands Master Korin. "This is the second time Lucifer has stepped foot on Earth in less than a year! He must be stopped!"

"I'm trying to put them at ease, Kor," Lady A. says. "They haven't told us everything yet."

There's no condemnation in her tone, but I still feel compelled to say something in our defense.

Mina speaks up before I can.

"The rest of the account isn't really our tale, but you need to hear it so we can present our request."

"What request?" demands Master Korin. "You are obligated to tell us the whole truth immediately."

Master Blaz raises a hand to shush him.

I stare at the ground to avoid glaring at Master Korin.

"Please continue," says Master Blaz. "Tell us what you held back, and then, we will hear your petition."

"We found Master Josiah."

Mina's announcement causes most Council members to speak at once. She pauses to give Master Blaz time to reestablish order.

"Where is he?" asks Master Blaz.

"He awaits your favor in another realm," Mina answers.

"What are you talking about, girl?" demands Master Korin. "Speak sense!"

"You must hear the rest to understand," says Mina, seemingly unfazed by Master Korin's ill-temper. "Master Josiah awaits with Lady Codee and their daughter in a place called Seriana."

"Leora." Lady A. whispers the name. "I thought Lucifer had destroyed her."

Her statement draws curious stares from Lady Deliah and

Master Titus.

"Elizabeth was never the same after she returned one day without her daughter or the bond with Josiah," Lady A. explains. "She couldn't even tell me what had happened."

"I knew they were close, but I didn't know they had a child," says Master Titus.

"Her name is Paige now," I say.

Master Blaz raises an eyebrow at the name but refrains from interrupting.

"Lucifer kidnapped her to draw out Master Josiah and Lady Codee," I add.

"It worked," Mina continues. "Lucifer wanted to steal their Kindred Spirit Bond, but something went wrong. Part of that event affected Lady Codee's abilities and memories and the rest split Master Josiah into two sections of spirit, one of body, and one of soul. I don't know how, but at least some of his spirit ended up in a diamond and becoming Spirit's Bane."

Everybody recognizes that name, but they cover the surprise well.

"I assume that means you destroyed the weapon?" Lady A.'s inflection makes it a question. "How did you accomplish this?"

"For a long time, I did not understand," Mina admits. "I thought Spirit's Bane was a weapon designed by Satan to destroy his enemies. That's the lie he told me. But the longer it stayed in me, the more familiar I became with the kinds of pain it caused and which situations would result in pain."

"What was the difference?" asks Master Blaz.

"I could use some spiritual gifts with only mild pain but turning to spirit or using certain Gifts had much greater consequences," Mina explains. "Eventually, I learned to see and experience the world in a new way. Master Josiah showed me a new plane of existence, a place for souls."

"Where are they? Why aren't they here to confirm this wild tale?" Master Korin's voice drips with irritation.

The reminder of the soul plane causes me to shift over to it. Each Council member blazes with inner light. I admit, I'm a little disappointed. The view shows me Master Korin's just a normal grump, not an evil one.

"That brings us to the request," says Mina, sidestepping the *where* question. "They would like to see the King."

"Not a chance until they stand before us," declares Master Korin.

"Can you be more specific?" Lady A. asks carefully. Her expression mirrors the wariness in every Council member. "Do you know what they intend to ask him?"

"Not for certain," Mina admits, "but Paige is vulnerable. They likely wish to seek his counsel on her behalf."

"She's the Academy infiltrator," Master Blaz muses. "One of them anyway."

"She needs our help," I say.

"Didn't you fight her several times, Allister?" Lady A. asks.

"I have," I answer, feeling the need to be formal.

"Yet, you make this request on her behalf. Why?" Lady A. presses.

I don't answer right away because it's not the sort of thing you rush into. I'm guessing that caution can be blamed on Mina's presence.

"I am not the King, so I do not know where any being stands concerning their loyalty," I say. "The Prince of Darkness cast Paige out because he sensed light in her. That must count for something."

"Given the same circumstances, I may have made the same choices she did," Mina adds.

"What circumstances?" asks Master Blaz.

"She was captured as an infant." Horror causes Lady A.'s voice to catch. "I can only imagine what Lucifer did to her."

"Does that have any bearing on the crimes she perpetrated against us?" asks Master Korin. "Have you forgotten the Academy attack already?"

"Nobody has forgotten," Lady A. assures her colleague, "but this does complicate matters by presenting us with a moral question."

"Let us summon her to stand trial," says Master Korin.

"I don't think Josiah and Elizabeth will let that happen," Lady A. notes. She waves toward Mina and me. "That is why these two are carrying the request to us."

"It doesn't matter," Master Korin argues. "They obviously know where to find the fugitives. Make them tell us."

"Let the King decide," suggests Master Titus.

"What if it's a trap?" demands Master Korin. "We have a duty to protect him."

Master Titus shrugs.

"The King is not helpless."

"It's not a trap," Mina declares. "Master Josiah and Lady Codee are broken and will need time to heal. Paige is hurt and confused. She has many questions. But I have also seen them through the soulscape. They are not evil."

"Paige as served Lucifer for many years." Master Blaz speaks the reminder gently. He raises a hand to hold back our protests. "Willingly or unwillingly can be determined later. The question remains: do we trust her enough to grant the request to see the King?"

Through great effort, I keep silent, knowing the question has been set before the other Council members. They contemplate the matter in silence.

Finally, Lady A. speaks.

"I do not know enough about this girl to render a fair judgment, but I trust Allister and Mina will be present at the meeting to render assistance as necessary."

Relief floods me.

"We will," I promise.

"Then you have my vote," Lady A. says.

Master Titus and Master Blaz echo her sentiment. Master Korin does not. We eagerly await Master Micah and Lady Deliah's opinions. Master Micah looks torn, but he eventually sides with Master Korin.

Lady Deliah watches Mina and me closely.

"Do you believe this girl would submit to precautionary measures?" she inquires.

"It would be a mistake," Mina says immediately. "She's been in too many kinds of chains for too long."

"Would she consent to being guarded by several Council members?" asks Master Blaz.

"That's the worst idea brought up yet," says Master Korin. "We'd only be giving her more targets to attack."

I want to silence him, but he raises a valid point.

"She might agree," Mina says, ignoring Master Korin's outburst. "I can ask her."

Lady Deliah nods once.

"Then under the condition that two Council members are within sight of the meeting at all times, you have my vote."

"Excellent. Now the hard part," says Master Blaz. "We need to decide which two representatives to send."

"Before we delve into that debate, we should finish the current discussion," Lady A. says. "Is there anything else you need to ask or add?" She looks expectantly at Mina and me.

I feel heat rising in my cheeks.

"The recent events have changed my perspective on a lot," Mina begins. She glances over at me before scanning each Council member. "Being immortal is not a guarantee of safety or success. Time is still precious, as are people."

"I love her," I say. Stepping up beside Mina, I entwine our fingers. "I know that's going to complicate our missions, but the Kindred Spirit Bond draws us together."

"We would like your permission to work and train together," Mina clarifies.

"Do you think that wise?" Master Blaz asks.

"Josiah and Elizabeth felt as you do," Lady A. reminds us.

"We are not them," Mina says, "but in the end, I believe their love for each other let them overcome every trial they faced."

Lady A. and Master Blaz exchange a quick look.

"Bring the matter up with the King," says Master Blaz. "If he approves, then so do we."

Epilogue:
Flowers

Case Report #: MN-130
Case Agents: Master Blaz and Mistress Codee
Guardian: Mina Nadir

While Master Blaz arranges for Allister and me to see the Glorious King, we spend a few hours in Mistress Clarimond's office giving her a more thorough version of our adventures. It feels like old times. We spent many a training day explaining ourselves to her at the Academy.

After our report, we discuss how to handle Master Josiah, Lady Codee, and Paige.

"It might be best to leave dealings with Josiah and Elizabeth to me," Lady A. says. "We have some history together. They may be more inclined to heed counsel if it comes from me."

"What will happen to them?" I wonder.

Lady A. shakes her head and lifts one shoulder in a shrug.

"That depends largely on how they answer the Council of Light's questions and what the King recommends."

"Are they in trouble?" Allister wonders. "Did they do something wrong?" His first question sounds curious. His second sounds nervous.

"They are not in trouble for falling in love, if that is your true question," Lady A. says, smiling to ease Allister. Her smile melts. "But they have made some questionable decisions with far-reaching consequences, and they will have to answer for

216

them."

"What happened to them?" Allister asks, leaning forward in his chair.

"I'm not sure exactly," Lady A. admits. "They took some time off to experience life as humans. The King had given them leave to take several years, so I hardly gave it another thought. I assumed everything was well with them."

"But it wasn't," Allister mutters.

Lady A. nods agreement.

"I learned of their daughter's existence when Elizabeth sent a frantic message about her being kidnapped."

Although Lady A.'s tone stays neutral, I see pain and regret etched around her eyes.

"Instead of going to them right away, I sent the message to the King." Her gaze drifts off to the past.

"The message never arrived," Allister guesses.

"My warning was intercepted," Lady A. confirms. "Demons waylaid me before I could reach the place where Elizabeth said she and Josiah would wait. They were gone by the time I arrived, and I didn't see them for many months. When they returned, nothing was the same between them, and Elizabeth seemed shattered. I didn't dare ask about their daughter." Lady A. releases a slow breath. "We lost touch for a long while after that. The only times I saw her were fleeting at best."

"That's sad," I say, "but you could not have known what truly transpired."

"The King did," Allister notes, "yet he said nothing."

"You can ask him why if you wish," Lady A. announces. "He's requested you meet him in Colorado with Paige."

"Alone?" Allister asks, sounding confused.

"Josiah and Elizabeth will have their own audience afterwards," Lady A. assures us. "For now, just you two and Paige."

Allister and I stand and instinctively reach for each other as we prepare to teleport to the meeting place.

"Do you have any last advice for us?" Allister wonders as our hands touch.

"Be honest and open to learning," Lady A. replies, "but also be prepared to fade into the background. Whatever decisions

Julie C. Gilbert

are made, Paige will need your love and support."

Bowing to acknowledge Lady A.'s advice, we teleport to the coordinates that appear in our minds simultaneously.

I expect to feel a stabbing sensation within my chest, but of course, nothing happens. As I draw my first breath of crisp, cold air, words appear in my mind's eye: **Blue Lakes Trail, Mount Sneffels Wilderness, Colorado**.

Surrounded by snow-covered trees, Allister and I pause to appreciate the beauty surrounding us. Our breaths billow out in foggy clouds. I glance around, considering that we might need to don more weather-appropriate gear to blend in.

"I think we're alone," Allister remarks. He slowly scans the nearby areas.

"Not completely," I say, gesturing to a clearing about a hundred feet away.

Paige stands under a tree, pacing back and forth. As we observe, her clothes flip from outdoor hiking gear to black armor to jeans and a green T-shirt. She changes her hairstyle to match each outfit. Sometimes it's tied back, but more often, the blond strands fly free in the gentle breeze coming off the lake behind her.

We begin walking toward her.

Before we arrive, Paige has tried a white dress, a red dress, and four more jeans and parka combinations.

At first, I'm amused by her indecision, but a glimpse of her expression steals the mirth.

Placing a hand on Allister's right shoulder, I halt our forward progress.

"Let me speak with her," I whisper.

Nodding solemnly, he steps aside to let me pass.

By the time I reach Paige, she's wearing black jeans and a dark gray long-sleeved T-shirt. Her hair is caught up in a simple ponytail.

"It doesn't matter what you wear," I say, approaching her slowly.

Paige shoots me an alarmed look, embarrassed at being observed in her indecision.

"Easy for you to say," she murmurs. "You always know where you stand."

"Not true," I argue, "but I do have the advantage of knowing the King longer than you. He'd want you to come as you are."

With a deep sigh, Paige hangs her head and shuffles some snow at her feet.

"That's the problem," she says. "I don't know who I am anymore."

"You are beloved." The declaration comes from my right and Paige's left. I'd recognize that voice anywhere. It's warm, inviting, powerful, and pleasant.

We drop to our knees and bow our heads, but not before I see what the King is wearing. He's in human form and standing in blue jeans and a black parka. Glory still shines from his face, but he diminishes it so we can comfortably stand in his presence.

My heart quickens its pace.

"I see you found a flower among the weeds, Mina," says the Glorious King. Stooping down, he picks up both of my hands and raises me to a standing position. After kissing my forehead, he lifts me up and spins me around in a quick circle. Joy radiates off him like waves of heat. "Well done and thank you!" He sets me on my feet and sobers. "I know the task was not easy."

Before my brain can work out a reply, the King releases me and raises Paige up beside me. He pulls her into a firm hug.

"Welcome, dear child." His voice wavers with thick emotion. "I have missed you."

Paige's emotional walls crumble and she sobs.

The King patiently waits for the tears to slow before speaking again.

"Release the past, dear one," says the King.

"But I've hurt so many people, both angels and humans!" cries Paige. She pulls out of his embrace.

"What was done in ignorance can be forgiven," answers the King.

"Why did you let me hurt so many?" Paige's question can barely be heard. Her hands form tight fists as she wrestles her emotions. "You could have stopped me."

"Every moment of your life has led you here," replies the King. "I offer you a home and a purpose, but I will not force any future upon you."

"But my parents. Mina. Allister. The countless humans." Paige shuts her eyes against the painful thoughts. "So much suffering." She drops to her knees again and lets more tears flow. "Am I worth it?"

Kneeling beside her, I wrap my arms around Paige.

To my surprise, the King kneels and embraces us.

"Absolutely," declares the Glorious King. "Do not worry about the others. Humanity has their savior, should they choose to accept the gift. And I have not asked anything of these others that they would not have willingly given."

I still my spirit as I feel the King's presence ministering to Paige and me. I'm not sure how long we stay like that, but eventually, the King lifts us to our feet again and waves Allister over. As he did with us, the King greets Allister with a holy kiss across his forehead and a warm, joyous embrace.

My favorite part is Allister's alarmed expression as the King twirls him around like he weighs nothing. Afterwards, he plants Allister next to me and places a hand on each of our shoulders, nudging us to stand closer together.

"What has started between you has my blessing," he says solemnly. "Let the Kindred Spirit Bond grow ever stronger each day. It is a sign of my authority and power entrusted to you, my faithful ones. Enjoy some rest. Then, be ready to work. There are many more flowers to find."

We spend some time listening to the King patiently answer Paige's many questions concerning her future. It's decided that she'll attend the Academy in a special capacity under the tutelage of a Council of Light member. I secretly hope she ends up with Master Korin because she'd challenge some of his stuffier beliefs. It would be good for him.

Eventually, the Glorious King sweeps Paige away so they can meet with Master Josiah and Lady Codee.

I'm slightly disappointed to be left out of that meeting until Allister slips his right arm around my waist, and I realize we're alone in a vast, beautiful winter landscape.

Twisting within his grasp, I rest my head on his chest.

"Do you think she'll be all right?" asks Allister, resting his chin on my head.

"Of course. She's with the King," I answer. "He can cure

her of the hurts she clings to."

"What about you?" Allister inquires. "Will you be all right? You've been through a lot."

"I too have the King to help me," I answer. Lifting my head, I grin at my friend. "And I have Master Blaz, Lady C., and Takoda to keep me grounded." Allister opens his mouth to promise his support, but I cut him off with a quick kiss. "And I have you to love and be loved by. That's enough for now."

THE END

Thank You for Reading:

This story gave me quite a few fits and took far longer than most other projects. It's also been covered in more prayer than most of my works. I hope you enjoyed taking this journey with me. It's 100% fantasy, but there is certainly a battle of good vs. evil raging around us.

Please visit my website: **www.juliecgilbert.com** to find a link to Spirit's Bane. There should also be a list of the current free works. Check out the stories in different mediums. The audiobooks have fantastic narrators, and the paperbacks have awesome covers by talented artists.

Join the Facebook group *Julie C. Gilbert's Special Agents* for news and giveaways.

Connect with me via email at **devyaschildren@gmail.com**.

Lastly, if you enjoyed the story, please leave a review at your favorite retailer. Thanks again.

Other Contacts:
www.facebook.com/JulieCGilbert2013
www.instagram.com/juliecgilbert_writer/
https://twitter.com/authorgilbert
www.bookbub.com/authors/julie-c-gilbert

www.ingramcontent.com/pod-product-compliance
Lightning Source LLC
Chambersburg PA
CBHW061138170626
46809CB00003B/903